"I need a favor. A big one. I need you to marry me. *Tonight*."

The look Jericho gave her let Laurel know that he thought she'd lost her mind. Maybe she had. But she didn't exactly have a lot of options, and Jericho was still her best bet.

"Marry you?" he repeated.

He was no doubt remembering the bad history between them. "What's going on?" He turned as if he was about to show her to the door but then stopped. And studied her with those cop's eyes. The warm amber-brown-colored eyes weren't so warm right now, but Laurel had firsthand knowledge that they could be.

Every part of Jericho could be *warm*.

Again, it was firsthand knowledge fed by years of experience of kissing him. Touching him, wanting him.

TAKING AIM
AT THE SHERIFF

USA TODAY Bestselling Author
DELORES FOSSEN

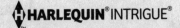

Recycling programs
for this product may
not exist in your area.

ISBN-13: 978-0-373-74926-3

Taking Aim at the Sheriff

Copyright © 2015 by Delores Fossen

All rights reserved. Except for use in any review, the reproduction or
utilization of this work in whole or in part in any form by any electronic,
mechanical or other means, now known or hereinafter invented, including
xerography, photocopying and recording, or in any information storage
or retrieval system, is forbidden without the written permission of the
publisher, Harlequin Enterprises Limited, 225 Duncan Mill Road,
Don Mills, Ontario M3B 3K9, Canada.

This is a work of fiction. Names, characters, places and incidents are
either the product of the author's imagination or are used fictitiously,
and any resemblance to actual persons, living or dead, business
establishments, events or locales is entirely coincidental.

This edition published by arrangement with Harlequin Books S.A.

For questions and comments about the quality of this book,
please contact us at CustomerService@Harlequin.com.

® and TM are trademarks of Harlequin Enterprises Limited or its
corporate affiliates. Trademarks indicated with ® are registered in the
United States Patent and Trademark Office, the Canadian Intellectual
Property Office and in other countries.

Printed in U.S.A.

Delores Fossen, a *USA TODAY* bestselling author, has sold over fifty novels with millions of copies of her books in print worldwide. She's received the Booksellers' Best Award and the RT Reviewers' Choice Best Book Award. She was also a finalist for a prestigious RITA® Award. You can contact the author through her webpage at dfossen.net.

Books by Delores Fossen

Harlequin Intrigue

Appaloosa Pass Ranch

> *Lone Wolf Lawman*
> *Taking Aim at the Sheriff*

Sweetwater Ranch

> *Maverick Sheriff*
> *Cowboy Behind the Badge*
> *Rustling Up Trouble*
> *Kidnapping in Kendall County*
> *The Deputy's Redemption*
> *Reining in Justice*
> *Surrendering to the Sheriff*
> *A Lawman's Justice*

The Lawmen of Silver Creek Ranch

> *Grayson*
> *Dade*
> *Nate*
> *Kade*
> *Gage*
> *Mason*
> *Josh*
> *Sawyer*

Visit the Author Profile page
at Harlequin.com for more titles.

CAST OF CHARACTERS

Sheriff Jericho Crockett—No one's ever accused him of being Mr. Nice Guy, but this tough cowboy cop has always had a blind spot when it comes to Laurel Tate. Now Laurel's back with a big secret—a child—and Jericho's the only thing standing between them and a killer.

Laurel Tate—Two years ago she walked out on Jericho because she thought it would save his life, but it only postponed the threat. Now the danger has returned with a vengeance, and it could cost her both Jericho and her son.

Maddox—The toddler at the center of a fierce custody battle. Maybe he's even the reason for the danger.

Herschel Tate—Laurel's father, who has some secrets of his own. He wants to raise his grandson, but just how far would he go to get custody?

Theo James—This businessman was once engaged to Laurel, and he plans to win her back with the promise that he can keep her and her son safe.

Dorothy James—Theo's mother and business partner. She makes no attempt to hide her hatred for Laurel, but she claims she's not behind the attacks that have sent Laurel on the run.

Chapter One

Sheriff Jericho Crockett didn't have time to react. The SUV flew out from the side road and slammed right into the side of his truck.

The jolt was instant, tossing him around, and the seat belt snapped like a vise across Jericho's body. It knocked the breath out of him and dazed him for a couple of seconds.

He couldn't say the same for the driver of the SUV.

No dazed moments for the person behind that heavily tinted windshield. The driver backed up a few yards and came at Jericho again. This time, the front end of the SUV collided with his pick-up's engine and then pulled back before coming onto the main road behind Jericho.

Much to Jericho's surprise, the guy didn't bolt. The SUV stayed put, the driver revving up the engine as if it were some kind of wild animal on the verge of pouncing for an attack.

What the hell was going on here?

Was someone trying to kill him? Or at least put him in the hospital? Jericho wasn't about to let either of those things happen. He drew his Smith & Wesson from his waist holster and threw open his door.

The blast of December air came right at him, spiking a chill in him that went bone deep. But the cold didn't stop him. Jericho leaned out just enough so that he'd still have some cover but so this clown would see his gun.

What Jericho still couldn't do was get a glimpse of the person inside. Of course, the darkness didn't help. Nor did the fact that the driver didn't even have on his headlights.

"I'm Sheriff Crockett!" Jericho shouted. "Get out of your vehicle now!"

Since this crazy attack had come out of the blue, Jericho wasn't sure what to expect, but he braced himself in case someone in that SUV tried to take shots at him.

But that didn't happen.

The SUV came at him again, slamming into the back of his truck and causing Jericho's arm and shoulder to bash against the steering wheel. He held on to his gun, thank God, and he used it. Jericho sent two bullets into the SUV's engine, but they ricocheted off. Obviously, it'd been reinforced in some kind of way, because the front fender wasn't even crushed.

"The next shot goes through the windshield," Jericho warned him. Easier than putting bullets through metal, anyway. "And right into you."

The warning must have worked because this time the guy didn't crash into him. The driver threw the SUV into Reverse and hit the accelerator, the tires kicking up smoke and stench as they squealed away.

Since this was a farm road, less than a quarter of a mile from Jericho's family ranch, there wasn't much traffic, but he didn't want an innocent bystander hit by someone who was either drunk or just plain dangerous. He was more than ready to go after the idiot, but the spewing steam from his engine stopped him. The radiator had probably been busted in the collision, and he wasn't going to get far. Best to try to get to the ranch and regroup.

Cursing, Jericho took out his phone and pressed his brother's number. Jax, who was a deputy and still at work, answered on the first ring.

"I think somebody just tried to kill me," Jericho said instead of a greeting. He eased his foot down on the accelerator, hoping the truck would make it home.

"Again?" Jax asked. It wasn't exactly a smart-mouthed question. Earlier in the day, Jericho had been shot at during a domestic dispute. Now, this.

"A black SUV rammed into me three times, tore up my truck and then drove off. Run the plates for me." Jericho rattled off the license numbers, and he heard the clicks his brother was making on the computer keyboard back at the sheriff's office in the nearby town of Appaloosa Pass.

"You okay?" Jax sounded considerably more concerned with this question than his last one.

"I'm fine." Well, except for what would no doubt be a god-awful bruise on his shoulder. It was already throbbing like a toothache.

"The plates aren't registered," Jax provided a moment later. "They're bogus."

Of course they were. "Find this moron and arrest his sorry butt. Once I'm at my house, I'll get another vehicle and help you look for him."

"I can handle this. No need for you—"

"I'll be there," Jericho insisted, and he ended the call.

Well, there went his plans for a quiet night. Dinner and sleep. Maybe not even in that order since he was fully spent after pulling a twelve-hour shift. But apparently his shift wasn't over. Yes, his brother could handle this. Jax could handle pretty much anything when it came to a lawman's work. But this was personal, and that meant Jericho would have his hands in it.

The truck engine continued to chug and spew

steam, but he was finally able to reach his place. Thankfully, it was at the front of the ranch property, the house that'd once belonged to his great-aunt and -uncle.

Jericho kept watch around him, just in case the bad-driving nut job returned, and he hurried up the back steps and into his kitchen so he could get the keys for his spare truck. He instantly spotted the note taped to his door.

"'I put up a tree for you. Love, Mom,'" he read aloud.

He automatically scowled. He wasn't much of a Christmas person. Definitely didn't put up trees—even though Christmas was only two days away. But he made a mental note to thank his mother, anyway.

Jericho stepped inside and cursed again once he turned on the lights and noticed the blood on his shirt.

Then, on his shoulder.

He peeled off his jacket and cowboy hat, dropping them on the table, and after he removed his badge, he sent the shirt flying straight toward the washer in the adjoining laundry room. It wasn't a deep cut, barely a nick, but it was bleeding enough that he'd need a bandage.

Jericho made it one step into the living room when he heard someone moving around.

And he put down his badge and drew his gun.

Great day in the morning, had the idiot in the SUV gotten here ahead of him?

"Jericho," a woman said. Her voice was a whisper.

He picked through the dark room and located her. Right next to a Christmas tree with all the trimmings. Even though he could barely see the brunette sitting on his sofa, he knew exactly who she was.

Laurel Tate.

She wasn't the very last person on earth that he would have expected to see in his house, but it was close. Jericho hadn't laid eyes on Laurel in over two years, since she'd moved from her father's nearby ranch to Dallas where she was supposed to run one of her family's businesses.

A shady one, no doubt.

Which pretty much described all her family's businesses.

Heck, Jericho's nights with her had been shady of a different sort since she was hands off. But those nights had been memorable, as well. He wasn't very happy about that. Wasn't happy about giving in to this scalding heat that'd always been between them.

Still was.

Much to his disgust.

"Nice tree," she remarked. "Your mother's doing?"

"Really? I doubt this visit is about Christmas

trees. Or my mother. Why are you here?" he growled. "And how'd you get in?"

She fluttered her fingers toward the back door. "It wasn't locked, and I had to see you, *alone*, so I didn't want to go to your office," Laurel said, as if that explained everything.

It didn't explain squat. "Well, you can use that same unlocked door to let yourself out. I don't have time for a visit."

Laurel got to her feet. Slowly. Her cool blue eyes fastened to him. Not just on his face, either. Her gaze slid over his upper body, reminding him that he was bleeding and shirtless. Jericho hoped it was the blood that caused her breath to go all shivery like that, because he wasn't the least bit interested in having her react to his body.

They were enemies now. But lovers once.

Okay, not just once.

They'd been sixteen when they'd first discovered sex together, in this very house the summer he'd been staying at the place when his great-aunt and -uncle had been away. Jericho had actually discovered sex a year earlier with the cute cheerleader whose name he couldn't remember, but he'd been Laurel's first. A first had turned to a second, third and so on until his father's murder two years later.

Things had changed big-time between them then.

Everything had changed.

But he damn sure remembered Laurel's name.

Every inch of her body, too. A reminder that Jericho told to take a hike.

"You're bleeding," she said.

"And you're leaving so I can take care of it." But then he got a bad thought. *Really bad.* "Did you have something to do with the guy in the SUV who ran into me? Let me rephrase that. Did your scummy father have anything to do with it?"

Because Laurel wasn't the sort to get her hands dirty. She just associated with the low-lifes who did.

Her eyes widened and she shook her head. "Someone tried to hurt you?" And yeah, it sounded like a genuine question from a concerned, surprised woman.

"Is your father responsible for my bloody shoulder and bashed-up truck?" he pressed.

It wouldn't have been Herschel Tate's MO to be so obvious. He was more a knife-to-the-back sort of guy. Too bad Jericho had never been able to pin any crimes on him. Especially one big crime.

The murder of Jericho's own father.

Twenty years later, the pain of that still cut him to the bone. And that pain spilled over onto Laurel because she'd refused to see the truth or help him put her murdering father behind bars.

"I don't think my father was involved with anything that happened to you tonight." Laurel shook her head again. "But I can't be positive."

Well, that was a first—having her admit that her precious daddy could do anything wrong. But Laurel didn't elaborate. She hurried past him, and for a moment Jericho thought she was leaving. Instead, she came back from the kitchen with some paper towels that she pressed to his shoulder.

Jericho eyed her. Her nursing attempt put her fingers in contact with his bare skin. "How'd you get here?" he snapped. "Did your father or somebody else drop you off?"

Though he couldn't imagine why Herschel would do that. The hatred Jericho felt for the man was mutual.

"No. My father doesn't know I'm here. No one does. I parked behind your barn."

Since he had a big driveway and side yard, there was only one reason to park behind the barn. To conceal the vehicle. Jericho couldn't think of a single good reason for her to do that, but since he was a cop, he could think of some bad ones.

"Start talking," he insisted.

Laurel didn't do that, though. She kept dabbing at the cut. And more. Now that she was this close to him, Jericho could see her bottom lip tremble a little. He could also see that the whites of her eyes had some red in them.

Had she been crying?

"Your hair's longer," she said, her breath hitting against his neck right next to the hair she was apparently noticing. "It suits you."

That earned her a flat stare, and to end the little touching session, Jericho snatched the paper towels from her. "Are you really here to chat about my infrequent trips to the barbershop?"

"No." She moved away from him, repeated her answer and tucked a strand of her own loose hair behind her ear. "But we need to talk."

"So you've said. Well, start talking. Jax is waiting on me to come back to the station so we can go after the guy who hit my truck."

Jericho made sure he sounded impatient enough. Because he was. But Laurel didn't seem to be in a hurry to start this conversation that he didn't exactly want to have. So, Jericho started it for her.

"If you're here on your father's behalf—to try to make some kind of truce or deliver a threat— I'm not in a truce-making or threat-listening kind of mood."

"It's not anything like that." Laurel paused, pulled in her breath. "It's about…marriage."

Jericho went still. The woman sure knew how to keep him surprised. After all, Laurel was already married. Or at least she was supposed to be. But now that he had a better look at her left hand, she wasn't sporting a flashy diamond or a wedding band.

She followed his gaze to her ring finger and shook her head. "I didn't go through with the wedding. I called it off." Laurel looked up at him, clearly waiting, as if she expected him to ask why.

He'd rather eat a magazine of bullets first. But if the gossip was right, Laurel was supposed to be married to one of her father's rich lackey lawyers. Considering that she, too, was an equally rich lackey lawyer, it was no doubt a match made in some place other than heaven.

"Look, Laurel, like I keep saying, this isn't a good time—"

The rest of what he was about to remind her just stopped there in his throat when she opened her hand, and Jericho saw the small blue stone. She'd obviously been holding it for a while, because there was a mark on her palm.

"You remember what this is?" she asked.

Yeah, he did. And while it would seem petty to deny that, Jericho nearly went with petty.

Nearly.

"It's the rock we found on the banks of Mercy Creek twenty years ago," he supplied.

"We went walking there after we, well,

afterward." Laurel tipped her head toward the bedroom, to the very place where she'd lost her virginity to him. "We found the two rocks. They were almost identical in size, shape and color. We'd never seen rocks that color before, so we decided it was some kind of sign, maybe even good-luck charms."

Jericho couldn't remember if he'd paid his electric bill this month, but he remembered that twenty-year-old conversation with Laurel. Every blasted word of it. And he knew that silly teenage notions of signs and charms like that came with a price tag attached.

"You said we'd each keep one, and that this rock could be a marker of sorts. Payment for any favor down the road. *Anything*," Laurel added. "In all these years, I've never used it because we said it should be for something very important. And we'd know just how important it was because we'd used this marker."

Jericho nodded. "I figured that'd come more in the form of a favor, like buying you a horse or something. Or if you needed me to whip somebody's butt for messing with you."

And then it hit him. What this visit might really be about. "You don't think we're going to make the same mistake again of having sex?" he asked.

"A mistake," she said under her breath. Not

exactly an agreement, but Jericho couldn't quite put his finger on the tone in her voice. And he certainly didn't see a let's-have-sex look in her eyes.

Not exactly, anyway. Of course, when it came to Laurel and him, there was always heat. Unwanted heat. But heat nonetheless.

"No. I'm not here for *that*," she verified.

"Good."

His body didn't exactly agree with that. Never did when it came to Laurel, but after that last fiasco together, Jericho had learned his lesson. Play with fire. Get burned. Or in their case, get burned *bad*, because for a couple of hours, it had made him forget her scummy family.

And Jericho had paid for it.

Hell, he was still paying.

It was a good reminder because it made Jericho realize it was time for Laurel to leave. However, before he could even point to the door again, Laurel took his hand and put the rock in it.

"I do need a favor. A big one." She swallowed hard. "Jericho, I need you to marry me. *Tonight*."

Chapter Two

Laurel wished she'd been able to come up with a better way to do this. Hard to come up with anything, though, with the tornado of emotions going on in her head. Of course, Jericho now had some emotions, too.

Bad ones, obviously.

Because the look he gave her let Laurel know that he thought she'd lost her mind. Maybe she had. But she didn't exactly have a lot of options here, and Jericho was still her best bet.

Even if he didn't believe that right now.

"Marry you?" Jericho repeated.

He was no doubt remembering the bad history between them. And he probably included their last one-nighter in that heap of bad history.

"It'll take more than a rock to make that happen." He cursed, dropped it on the table. "What's going on here?"

Laurel had figured that would be his first response—anger and demands. It was certainly hers when this idea had first come to her. Still, she was hoping the blue rock and the promise that had gone along with it would buy her enough time so she could explain things before Jericho kicked her out.

No such luck.

He turned as if he was about to show her to the door, but then stopped. And studied her with those cop's eyes. The warm amber-brown color wasn't so warm right now, but Laurel had first-hand knowledge that they could be.

Every part of Jericho could be *warm*.

Again, it was firsthand knowledge fed by years of experience of kissing him. Touching him, wanting him. And then having that warmth vanish and cool to iceberg temperatures like those outside right now.

Well, except for that night over two years ago.

Those two years seemed like a lifetime. For her, anyway. Jericho looked the same except for the slightly longer brown hair. In other words, he still looked like the hot cowboy he'd always been. Maybe it was his DNA, those eyes or the fit of his jeans, but when a woman saw Jericho Crockett, she noticed.

Laurel had been no different.

"I need an explanation," he pressed. "Like right now."

Where to start?

She doubted Jericho would want her to get into the little details. Not just yet, anyway. Judging from the impatient stare, he was looking for the condensed version of why she'd called in a very old marker that to him was probably worthless.

Laurel picked up the rock, slipped it into the front pocket of his jeans, careful not to touch too much of him.

"I had a baby," she finally said. "A son named Maddox. And my father is challenging me for custody."

It crushed her to say that.

Crushed her even more to think that her father might succeed.

The tears came again, and Laurel tried to blink them back. She'd already cried an ocean of tears, and they didn't help. Now she had to focus on a fix for this. She had to do whatever it took to save her son.

"A baby?" His gaze skimmed over her body. "You don't look like you've had a kid. And the gossips around town sure haven't gotten hold of that tidbit."

"I guess being several hundred miles away has kept the gossips from putting their noses in my business." Added to that, she'd worked very hard to make sure the news stayed within her family and a very small circle of friends.

For all the good that'd done her.

Jericho huffed, and his hands went on his hips. "So, your father's challenging you for custody, huh? Guess that means you two had some kind of falling-out. Or maybe you finally learned what a sack of dirt he really is."

"I've always known." She let that hang in the air for a few moments. "But I stayed for my mother's sake. As sort of a buffer between him and her."

He studied her. With some obvious skepticism in his gaze. There was a reason for that. Laurel had indeed defended her father over the years. Had believed his lies when he'd told her that his businesses would all be legitimate. Most of his lies, anyway.

And even that little shred of belief had cost her, big-time.

It'd cost Laurel her freedom. Her safety. It'd also cost her Jericho. What she needed to tell him wouldn't help, either.

"My mother had cancer and passed away," Laurel said. "She died two weeks ago."

"I'm sorry. Losing a parent is hard." The look of sympathy that he gave her was genuine, but it didn't last. "I'm guessing after her death was when things fell apart with your father?"

"More or less." Mainly *less*, but she'd save that for another time. "I don't think it'll come as a surprise to you that my father has influence over several judges. Doctors and psychiatrists, too. He's trying to declare me mentally and morally incompetent to raise my son. There's no truth to it," she added, just in case Jericho doubted it.

Which he probably did.

But he also no doubt believed that her father wasn't competent to raise Maddox, either.

Jericho stayed quiet a moment. "And you think if you're married, *to me*, that your father will… what? Step back from this fight he has with you? Herschel's never backed off from anything, period."

Her father wouldn't do that this time, either. Unless he had no choice. She had to make sure he didn't get that choice.

Because she needed it, Laurel took a moment, too. "If we're married, I'd sign over custody to you. Immediately. My father might have enough dirt on me to declare me incompetent, but he can't do the same to you."

She hoped.

After all, Jericho had been the sheriff of Appaloosa Pass for well over a decade. He was respected by some. Feared by others. It would be next to impossible to fabricate enough to smear his reputation, and Laurel was hoping a corrupt judge would back down from trying to go after Jericho.

"What kind of dirt does Herschel have on

you?" he asked. Of course, Jericho wasn't going
to let that slide.

"My father manufactured some of it. Some of
it was my own stupidity in handling one of his
business accounts."

And again, that was an explanation best saved
for another day. She hadn't done anything know-
ingly, but she had known her father. Had known
what he was capable of doing. Now that her father knew the whole truth, he would use anything to hurt her where it hurt the most.

By going after Maddox.

Jericho's stare got worse. So did his profanity.
"Surely there's somebody other than me who can
do this for you. Like your ex-fiancé?"

"He can't help," she settled for saying. And, in
fact, he was a big part of the problem.

"Really? You'd think the kid's father would
have something to say about you asking another
man to marry you." A muscle flickered in his
jaw. "What's your ex's name, anyway? Leo-
something-or-other."

"Theo James," she supplied.

Jericho lifted his right eyebrow. "Oh, I get it
now. Theo doesn't have a clean record, either,
and your father will use that to get custody of his
only grandson." His eyebrow went higher. "You
probably should have picked a different guy to
hook up with, Laurel."

She had. And Laurel would have told Jericho that, too, if the sound hadn't shot through the room. Since her nerves were already right there at the surface, she gasped, her body readying itself to fight yet another battle.

But it was just Jericho's phone.

"It's Jax," he said, and quickly answered it.

Even though Jericho didn't put the call on speaker, Laurel was close enough to hear what Jax told him. "We caught the guy in the SUV. He was on the side of the road trying to switch out the bogus plates. I'm bringing him in now."

The news caused Jericho's shoulders to relax a little, but that quickly ended when his gaze snapped back to her. "Good," he said to his brother. "Has he said anything about why he did it?"

"Not a word. He's already lawyered up, but I'll see if I can get anything from him."

"I want to talk to him," Jericho insisted. "I won't be long. Laurel Tate's here, and I need to finish up some things with her."

Jax paused. For a long time. "Laurel," he repeated, the venom clearly in his voice. "Why the heck is she at your place?"

"You wouldn't believe me if I told you."

No, he wouldn't. Nor would Jax approve. Because like the rest of the Crocketts, Jax blamed her in part for his father's death. They'd never forgive her for that.

Laurel wouldn't forgive herself, either.

She wouldn't forgive herself for a lot of things.

Jax cursed, and she had no trouble hearing it. "Please tell me you're not getting mixed up with Laurel again," he said to Jericho.

"No." Jericho didn't hesitate. Of course, Laurel had known he wouldn't simply agree to marry her. But hopefully he would when he understood the big picture.

She could practically see Jax's puzzled expression, but he didn't press things. "I'll see you when you get here."

And at that time, Jax would no doubt want a full explanation as to why their enemy's daughter was in his brother's house.

Jericho pushed the end call button and walked right past her. First to the kitchen so he could retrieve his badge from the counter. Then, toward his bathroom, she quickly realized, when she followed him.

"Look, I sympathize with this problem you're having with your father," he said, taking a bandage from the medicine cabinet. "Herschel shouldn't be raising any kid. But I can't help you." Jericho slapped the bandage on his shoulder and then went into his bedroom.

She followed him there, too.

Even though there were dozens of things on her mind, important things, Laurel still felt the punch from the old memories here. The room hadn't changed much in the twenty-two years since she'd been here for the first time.

Since she'd landed in that bed with Jericho.

Laurel made the mistake of looking at him before she could rein in the heat that trickled through her. A big mistake. Because Jericho saw that heat, and he scowled at her.

"My answer's not going to change," he insisted, taking a gray shirt from the closet. Once he had it on, he clipped on his badge. "It doesn't matter what happened between us on that bed. Or what happened over two years ago."

Laurel was about to tell him that it did indeed matter, but this time it was her phone that rang. She took it from her pocket, and when she saw her father's name on the screen, she let it go to voice mail—along with the other dozen messages he'd left her in the past couple of hours. She didn't have to listen to the message to know what he was demanding again.

That she hand Maddox over to him.

Or else agree to every detail of his sick plan.

She didn't intend to do either one of those.

"I can't let him get his hands on my son," she whispered.

"Good luck with that." It sounded like a dismissal, but she thought she saw some concern in Jericho's eyes. "I take it you've hidden the baby so that Herschel can't find him?"

She nodded. "He's with a friend I trust."

"A friend," he repeated, that cop's stare coming at her again. "But I'm guessing this is a friend who can't help you with your marriage problem."

"No."

He huffed, scrubbed his hand over his face. "I can't do this. What I can do is make some calls and arrange a safe house where you can stay until you work things out with Herschel. For now, I need to get to the station to question this dirt-for-brains suspect."

Yes, Jericho had made it crystal clear that he had more important things to do and no intention of helping her. So, Laurel pulled out the big guns. Or rather, the picture. It was the screen saver on her phone, and she held it up for him to see.

"That's my son, Maddox," she said.

Laurel didn't need to see the picture to be able to describe it in complete detail. The precious little boy with the blondish-brown hair, amber eyes and a melt-your-heart kind of smile.

Not a newborn baby.

As Jericho had likely been expecting.

Since Laurel was watching him so closely, she saw the change in his expression when he began to connect the dots. It wasn't a huge change. Just the muscles in his face going tight for a moment. Followed by a head shake, and then that lethal stare came back to her.

"How old is he?" Jericho asked. Except it wasn't just a question. It was a demand spoken through clenched teeth, and he practically ripped the phone from her hand for a closer look at the picture.

Laurel tried to steel herself for what was no doubt about to be a fierce storm. "He's eighteen months."

There. That was the last bit of information that Jericho needed so he could finally understand why she'd had come to him. Why their marriage had to happen and happen fast.

Why she couldn't turn to anyone else.

"Yes," Laurel verified. Her voice cracked, and she had to clear her throat before she could continue. "Maddox is your son."

Chapter Three

The blood rushed to Jericho's head.

It happened too fast for him to get hold of himself before it felt as if someone had slugged him with a hammer.

So many emotions went through him. The shock. The anger. The feeling that his life had just turned on a dime.

Because it had.

Everything had just turned.

Laurel and he had been together two years and three months ago, the perfect timing for them to have an eighteen month old son.

"Why?" he managed to say, though it would be the first of many questions. Questions that Laurel had darn sure better be able to answer.

Laurel didn't exactly jump to answer, but then she didn't back away from him, either. Even though he had to be giving her his worst glare, she held her ground.

"You should probably sit down," she suggested.

No way would sitting help. Nothing could at this point. His entire body was a tangle of nerves and fresh adrenaline—all caused by that picture of the little smiling face on Laurel's phone.

Everything about that face was familiar.

Because it was practically identical to pictures he'd seen of himself when he was a baby.

"Why?" he repeated, his jaw so tight now that he was hurting.

"I didn't tell you because I didn't want my father to find out. I was afraid he would kill you."

"He would have tried," Jericho conceded. Now the profanity came, and he couldn't stop himself from cursing Laurel. "You still should have told me."

Her chin dropped a little, and while she still held her ground, the tears shimmered in her eyes again. He wasn't immune to those tears, but right now he had no intention of giving Laurel one ounce of comfort.

How dare she do this.

"I already had your father's death on my conscience," she said. "I didn't want your death there, too."

"That's no excuse." He jabbed his index finger at her and considered punching the wall just to release some of this dangerous energy revving up inside him. Hardly a mature reaction, but this had shaken him to the core.

A baby!

Except he wasn't exactly a baby now. He was eighteen months old. Born nine months after Laurel and he had ended up in bed. And she'd kept it from him this entire time.

"You had no right," he warned her.

"Maybe not, but what's done is done. I'm sorry I can't give you more time to come to terms with this. I'm sorry about a lot of things. But right now, we have to stop my father from taking him."

Jericho got a new surge of anger, too. Except this was more rage, and it was aimed at Herschel. "That won't happen. No way will I let that snake take custody of..." But the words wouldn't come so he could finish that.

My son.

However, it was exactly what Jericho meant. It wasn't happening. It already sickened him to realize that Herschel had been part of the little boy's life this entire time.

And that Jericho hadn't been.

Later, he'd *address* that with Laurel.

"Why is Herschel trying to take custody?" Jericho asked. "*How* is he trying to do it?" he amended.

"My father has two fake psychiatric reports on me," Laurel explained. Not easily. The words seemed to stick in her throat. "Both claiming that I'm mentally unstable."

"You could counteract those with your own real psychiatric reports." Because Laurel had been careless and irresponsible when it came to her father, but she wasn't crazy.

"I could, but I don't own the judge that'll be presiding over the hearing. Plus, my father has a document I signed that's connected to some illegal funds that were transferred from an offshore account. I did sign it, but I had no idea it was a part of a money laundering scheme."

So, Herschel was coming at her from two angles, but it did surprise Jericho there was only one document with her signature on it that could have criminal ties. After all, Laurel had worked for her father for nearly a dozen years, and she'd no doubt come in contact with plenty of his dirty businesses and schemes.

"I want the names of every person involved in that deal," Jericho insisted.

Laurel nodded, but there was plenty of hesitation in her expression. "My father said if I came to you for help, that he'd only make things worse for both of us."

Yeah, that sounded like Herschel. A man of threats. Though he didn't know how much harder her father could make things, considering he was trying to take Laurel's child.

Jericho's child, too.

The reminder didn't settle easily in his mind. Of course, nothing about this would.

"You don't doubt he's yours?" she asked.

"No." How could he? The proof was right there in front of him. "How much does Herschel know about Maddox's paternity?"

"Everything. *Now*," she added in a whisper. "At first, I'd told him Theo was Maddox's father, and Theo went along with it. But when I broke off the engagement, Theo told him the truth. That's why Herschel wants custody right away. You know how much he hates you, and he hates me even more now that he knows I kept the truth about Maddox from him."

Jericho was betting there was a whole other story to go along with that one. Theo had probably squealed to get back at Laurel. He didn't know this Theo idiot, but he'd settle things with him later.

With Herschel, too.

Not just for this stunt he was trying to pull with getting custody, but because it was possible that Herschel had indeed been behind the hit-and-run idiot that Jax now had in the holding cell. Jericho didn't know exactly what Laurel's father would hope to gain by that, but anything was possible when it came to Herschel.

Especially anything illegal.

"Your father must have seen the resemblance

between Maddox and me," Jericho said, handing her back the phone.

"He did," Laurel readily admitted. "He didn't know about that night we were together. I'd managed to keep that from him, but he asked me point-blank if I'd been with you. I denied it, and I falsified the results of Maddox's paternity test so I could try to get him off your trail."

Jericho hadn't wanted Herschel off his trail. Especially not for something like this, something that would keep Maddox from him. The best way to deal with a snake was to confront it.

"Where's Maddox now?" Jericho asked.

"With a friend, Sandy Singer. She's a former cop, and she took him to her parents' house in Sweetwater Springs. Her parents are out of town so the place was empty."

So, Maddox was about thirty miles away. Close. But any distance wouldn't have mattered.

"I want to see him." And the glare Jericho gave Laurel dared her not to refuse him.

She didn't refuse him, though. She gave a shaky nod. "We'll just have to make sure we aren't followed."

He would make certain of that because he wouldn't put it past Herschel to take the boy, all in the name of keeping him safe from Laurel. Later, Jericho would have to do something about those false reports, but for now he had a more immediate problem on his hands.

"I have to call Jax and tell him I won't be able to question the man in custody until, well, until later," he settled for saying. Because Jericho had no idea how much time he'd need to start fixing this mess Herschel had created.

That Laurel had created, too.

"I'm sorry," she repeated, no doubt after she saw the latest round of anger go through his eyes.

Not in the mood for an apology that wouldn't help one bit, Jericho waved her off and took out his phone to call his brother. However, he stopped when he heard the sound.

A vehicle was approaching the house.

"Oh, God," Laurel whispered, her fingertips going to her mouth.

"It might be nothing," he assured her.

After all, his family's ranch was huge, and people came and went all the time. It could be one of the ranch hands, his mother or maybe even his sister, Addie, and her fiancé, Weston. Since Addie was pregnant, they were often making night runs to get whatever she was craving.

Heck, it could even be one of his other brothers, Levi or Chase. Both had houses on the grounds of the ranch.

"Wait here," Jericho told her, and he headed to

the living room window to look out. He braced himself for the worst.

And the worst was exactly what he got.

The moment he pulled back the curtain, he spotted the man who'd stepped from the black car now stopped in front of Jericho's house. It was dark enough that Jericho couldn't make out the guy's face, but he had no trouble seeing his gun.

Or hearing it.

The bullet slammed into the windowsill just a couple of inches from where Jericho was standing.

"Get down!" he shouted to Laurel.

But he did something to make sure that happened. Jericho hurried to her, hooked his arm around her waist and pulled her to the floor behind the couch. It wouldn't be much protection against bullets, but it was safer than her standing in a room with windows on the front and side.

"Call Jax for me," he said, tossing Laurel his phone. "I need backup and everyone in the main house warned that we're under attack."

Despite Laurel yelling for him to stay down, Jericho headed back to one of the windows so he could figure out who this idiot was and how to stop him.

From what Jericho could tell, the guy was alone. At least he was the only one out of the car. Of course, someone could be inside, waiting, so that's why he went to the window on the other side of the room. He wanted as much of an element of surprise as he could manage when he fired at this nut job. Maybe the guy wouldn't see him before Jericho got off the finishing shot.

"Jax is on the way," Laurel relayed to him. "He's bringing one of the deputies with him. Dexter Conway. He'll also call your mother and the rest of your family on the drive over."

Good. It'd take at least twenty minutes for Jax and Dexter to arrive, but maybe the attack was confined to just here. He didn't want Herschel's brand of violence spreading to the rest of his family.

"Now, please get down," Laurel added. "I'm calling Sandy to make sure everything is okay with Maddox."

Even though what Laurel was saying was important, Jericho shut her out, knocked out the pane of glass with his gun and took aim. He pulled the trigger, and though he couldn't be sure, he thought he might have hit the shooter in the shoulder. The guy ducked down and jumped into the car. Just in case he intended to get back out, Jericho sent another shot his way.

"Do you know for sure who's doing this?" Jericho asked Laurel.

"No. My father hates me now, but I can't believe he'd try to kill me."

"Believe it," Jericho said just as he got another surprise of the night.

Another bullet came right at him. Not from the idiot in the car this time. This shot had come from somewhere across the road. The land was level pasture there, and it would have been easy for a gunman to stand out, which meant the guy was likely hiding in the ditch.

Had he come with his partner in the car?

Probably.

Herschel no doubt wanted some kind of backup to make sure this attack was a success. After all, if Herschel got rid of both of Maddox's parents, then there'd be no fight for custody. However, that only led Jericho to yet another set of questions.

Did Herschel really want Maddox enough to kill for him?

And why?

Because Jericho wasn't sure a man like Herschel was capable of loving a child this much.

Jericho didn't have time to dwell on that because another shot came crashing through the window, and it spewed broken glass all over the room. Some of it even flew behind the couch.

Worse, it didn't stay a single shot.

The bullets began to rip through what was

left of the window. Tear through the walls, too. It was an old house with a wood frame, and if the shooters were using the right kind of bullets, they could do some serious damage before Jax and backup could even arrive.

"Crawl to my bathroom," Jericho told Laurel. "Get in the tub."

"You can't stay out here, either," she insisted.

"I'll be right behind you."

Maybe. But he immediately had to rethink that *maybe* when he finally spotted the shooter in the ditch. Jax would be there soon, and this guy was right next to the road. Jericho didn't want his brother getting hurt. Losing one family member to Herschel's schemes was more than enough.

Jericho moved to the side of a bookcase. Like the couch, it wasn't ideal coverage, but it would do. Hopefully. Since there wasn't any glass remaining in the window, he leaned out and fired right at the shooter in the ditch.

The guy dropped back down. But Jericho didn't think he'd managed to hit him.

Still, if he could keep both of these idiots pinned down, that would keep Laurel and the rest of the ranch safe. That thought had barely crossed his mind, however, when he heard a sound he definitely didn't want to hear.

More shots.

Coming from the car.

Shooter number one was back at it again, and this time the bullets weren't coming at Jericho. They seemed to be going on the other side of the house. Right in the direction of the bathroom where he'd just sent Laurel. And right in the direction of where there were sounds of yet more broken glass.

It didn't help when he heard her scream.

"You can't do this!" Laurel shouted. "Please. No!"

Hell.

Jericho raced from the living room, praying that one of those bullets hadn't hit her or that a third gunman hadn't managed to get into the house. Either was possible. He didn't have a security system and rarely even locked the windows or doors. Anyone could have gotten in.

Jericho kept as low as he could when he approached the bathroom. The light wasn't on, but there was a small window near the ceiling, and it gave him just enough illumination to see Laurel in the tub.

She had her left hand covering her head, and there were shards of glass on her from the broken window.

"Are you hit?" Jericho asked.

Her breath was gusting, and when she turned to look at him, that's when he saw that she had her phone against her ear. Despite the fact the bullets were coming at them nonstop, she still got out of the bathtub and would have bolted out the door if Jericho hadn't caught her.

"What's wrong?" he demanded, and he pulled her to the floor to get her out of the path of those shots.

Laurel frantically shook her head, fighting to get away from him. "They went after Maddox."

That handful of words sent his stomach straight to his knees. "Who did?"

"Kidnappers." Her answer rushed out with her breath, and Laurel scrambled to her feet again. "We have to get to him. Sandy said the kidnappers broke into her house, and they're trying to take Maddox right now."

Chapter Four

Laurel tried to push Jericho aside so she could run to her car. It didn't work. He held on, cursing at her to stop.

"Is your friend alone in the house with Maddox?" Jericho asked. "Has she called the Sweetwater Springs' cops?"

Laurel nodded to both his questions and tried to break free again. Everything inside her was spiraling out of control, and she was within a breath of a panic attack—something that wouldn't do her or Maddox any good—but she couldn't seem to stop herself.

"Getting yourself killed won't help Maddox," he snarled.

That helped with the panic. Well, it helped enough so that she could level her breathing and try to fight through the need to run.

Jericho took her by the arm and maneuvered her toward the kitchen. He slapped off lights along the way, pausing only long enough to put on his jacket and grab a set of keys before they went to the back door.

"Keep low and move fast," he ordered.

The relief flooded through her. They weren't going to hunker down and wait. They were going after Maddox. But that relief was short-lived when they stepped outside, and the bullets came. Not directly at them. The shooter was still firing into the front and side of the house, but without the walls to buffer the sounds, the shots were deafening.

And worse.

The shots started coming toward them.

"They're using infrared," Jericho said under his breath.

Someone obviously wanted them dead, but Laurel couldn't give in to the fear and panic that was snapping at her like the bitter wind. She had to get to Maddox.

Obviously, Jericho felt the same way because despite the shots, he practically dragged her onto the porch with him. With his hand on her back, he kept her low. Kept her running, too, toward his truck that was parked between them and the barn. That's when Laurel spotted the other damaged truck by the side of the house.

Soon, very soon, she'd need to find out if her father was responsible for that attack and this one. But for now, she had more pressing matters.

Jericho threw open the driver's side of his truck, shoving her inside and onto the floor. He shut the door, and in the same motion, he started the engine.

"Call Jax again." He tossed her his phone and hit the accelerator. "Tell him what's going on. And stay down."

Despite her shaking hands, Laurel found Jax's number in the recent calls and pressed it. "I'm almost there," Jax greeted her.

Laurel was about to tell him they were on the run, but the bullet blasted through the side window. The safety glass held, but it wouldn't for long.

"We're on our way to Sweetwater Springs," she said to Jax. "You need to get all the help you can out to 225 Anderson Lane to stop a kidnapping."

"A kidnapping? What's going on there?" Jax asked. At least he didn't hesitate, or curse her, after hearing her voice.

"Someone's trying to take…my son." Not exactly a lie, but Jericho would have to explain the full truth later: that Maddox was his son, too.

Now Jax cursed. Maybe because he'd already filled in the blanks or maybe because he had a child of his own and knew that this was a parent's worst nightmare.

"I'll make the call and get every available-lawman in the area out there." And Jax cursed some more when another bullet slammed into the truck. A bullet that he no doubt heard. "Tell Jericho to be careful," he added before he ended the call.

She relayed all of that to Jericho, emphasizing the last part. Did he listen? Of course not. And she was partially thankful for that. She didn't want Jericho hurt, but she also didn't want to waste any time getting to Maddox.

"Hurry," she said purely out of frustration.

Jericho was already hurrying, because she heard the tires squeal against the asphalt as he took a turn. Likely the one to the main road that would lead them to Sweetwater Springs. It was cold, just below freezing, and it was possible there was some ice on the roads. That didn't help the panic, either, but she was thankful that Jericho didn't slow down.

"Are they following us?" Laurel asked.

A muscle flickered in his jaw. "Yeah."

They couldn't lead the gunmen straight to Sandy's house. Of course, it was highly likely that both the gunmen and the kidnappers were working for the same person.

Her father.

"This is all my fault," she whispered. "I should have never left Maddox with Sandy."

"Herschel knows who Sandy is?" Jericho asked without taking his attention off the road.

"No, my father doesn't know her, but he must have found out about her." Laurel hadn't expected that. Especially not so soon. She'd only left Maddox with Sandy a little over two hours ago, and she hadn't thought anyone was following her.

She'd clearly thought wrong.

And her precious son could suffer because of her mistake.

"If Herschel's the one behind this," Jericho said, "then he won't hurt Maddox. Will he?" His jaw muscles tightened again, and there was a low, dangerous tone to that question.

"No. Not intentionally." But her baby was in the middle of an attack, and plenty of things could go wrong. Especially since both Sandy and the kidnappers would be armed, and Sandy wouldn't just let the kidnappers take Maddox without putting up a fight.

Oh, God.

Those hired guns could hurt Sandy. Or kill her. Her father would have given them orders to keep Maddox safe, but he wouldn't have extended such an order to the woman hiding his grandson.

Even though Jericho didn't say anything to her, Laurel could almost feel him trying to work out some kind of plan. Good. Because they needed something—anything—to save their son. No, her father wouldn't hurt Maddox, but if he got his hands on Maddox, he would hide him away so she could never find him.

"Hold on," Jericho warned her. "I have to do something about these SOBs behind us."

He slammed on the brakes, turning the steering wheel and bringing the truck to a stop sideways on the road. Laurel couldn't see the men following them, but she heard the squeal of their brakes as they approached. Felt the cold blast of air when Jericho lowered his window. He took aim.

Then, nothing.

Jericho just waited. The seconds crawling by. Precious time that they should be using to get to Maddox. Laurel knew they didn't have a choice. They couldn't arrive at Sandy's house with gunmen on their tail, but the waiting only caused the panic to smother her again.

Her heartbeat was already crashing in her ears. Her chest so tight that she couldn't breathe. But she could think, and her mind was coming up with all sorts of worst-case scenarios.

Even though she knew Jericho wouldn't approve, she lifted her head just enough so she could see out the side mirror. Laurel immediately spotted the black car. The passenger's door opened, and a man leaned out. He had a gun, and he pointed it right at them.

The shot blasted through the air.

It took her several heart-stopping moments to realize the gunman hadn't fired the shot. Jericho had. And their attacker dropped, falling out of the car and onto the ground.

Jericho fired another shot, this one slamming into the windshield right in front of the driver. The glass was tinted and there wasn't much of a moon, so she couldn't tell if the bullet hit the guy or not. Jericho maybe couldn't tell, either, because he sent two more shots in the same spot.

Nothing.

"Which word of *stay down* didn't you hear me say?" Jericho snarled. He didn't even spare her a glance, but he threw his truck into gear and got them moving again—fast.

She'd heard every word just fine, but Laurel had to see for herself if the gunmen were going to follow them. They didn't. Much to her relief, the black car didn't move when Jericho sped away.

Laurel got back down but gasped when another sound shot through the truck, and for one terrifying moment she thought the gunmen had returned fire, after all. But it was just Jericho's phone that she still had gripped in her hand.

"It's Jax," she said, glancing at the screen. Laurel answered the call and put it on speaker.

"I'm not far behind you—" Jax started.

"Look out for the black four-door car that's maybe still in the middle of the road near the creek," Jericho interrupted. "The guys inside are the ones who attacked Laurel and me."

"Did you kill them?" Jax asked.

"Maybe. But even if I didn't, I doubt they're in any shape to drive."

Good. It seemed wrong to celebrate anyone being shot or killed, but the men were another obstacle they didn't need.

"If they're alive," Jericho continued, "arrest them. Get answers from them and get them fast. But be careful. I don't know what kind of orders they have."

Neither did Laurel, but she did know that wounded men could still kill, and she didn't want that happening to Jax and Dexter.

"I'll keep an eye out for the men and the car," Jax assured him. "I just got off the phone with Sheriff Cooper McKinnon over in Sweetwater Springs. He and two deputies are at the residence. Two men fled on foot, and the deputies are in pursuit."

"Did they take Maddox?" Laurel couldn't ask fast enough.

"They didn't have a baby with them, but Cooper said he'd call me back once he was sure the residence was secure. I'll let you know as soon as I hear anything." And Jax hung up.

Her stomach tightened. It wasn't over. Just because those would-be kidnappers were running, it didn't mean there weren't other hired guns inside the house. Maybe holding Sandy and Maddox hostage.

Or worse.

"Don't go there," Jericho warned her. The glance he gave her this time let her know that he didn't want to deal with a hysterical woman. "You said your friend was a former cop, and I'm guessing she can handle herself or you wouldn't have left Maddox with her."

Laurel managed to nod. Sandy could indeed handle herself. But that didn't mean something couldn't have gone wrong. She should have hired a team of bodyguards to help, but there hadn't been time.

Maybe still wasn't.

"Any chance we'll be able to link any of these hired guns to your father?" Jericho asked.

"No chance whatsoever. My father is thorough." Among other things. She'd always known he was capable of breaking the law, but Laurel hadn't realized until recently just how far he would go to make sure he got what he wanted.

And what he wanted was Maddox.

"Now that I've defied him," she said, "my father will stop at nothing. *Nothing*," Laurel repeated.

Jericho stayed quiet a moment. Kept driving, the tires squealing when he took the curves too fast. "And you really think marriage will stop him?"

"No," Laurel readily admitted. "He'll put me in jail or a mental hospital. But what the marriage can do is prevent him from taking Maddox."

She hoped.

Still, it was a long shot. And judging from the way Jericho's forehead bunched up, she hadn't convinced him this was the way to go.

"Hang on," he said just as he took another sharp curve. The truck went into a skid, but Jericho quickly regained control.

Laurel was far enough down on the seat that she couldn't see out the windshield, but she did see the lights filtering in. No doubt from the town of Sweetwater Springs. That meant they were only minutes from Sandy's parents' house. However, it seemed to take an eternity for those minutes to pass.

She finally saw the swirl of blue lights from a police cruiser. Red lights, too. Probably from an ambulance.

That put her heart right back in her throat.

Laurel sat up, her gaze firing all around while

she tried to spot Maddox and Sandy. No sign of them, but she'd been right about the cruiser and the ambulance. Both were in front of Sandy's parents' house, and there were several lawmen milling around in the yard.

Before Jericho even pulled the truck to a full stop, Laurel tried to bolt out, but as he'd done at the house, he caught onto her arm and stopped her.

"I have to get to Maddox," she insisted.

"No. You have to wait here," he ordered. "And I mean it."

With his gun already drawn, Jericho threw open the door and made a beeline toward the tall, lanky man on the porch. Laurel recognized him—Sheriff Cooper McKinnon. Like Jericho, Cooper had had some run-ins with her father, but she hoped that wouldn't prevent him from doing his job and saving Maddox.

Laurel did wait in the truck. Several painful seconds. As long as she could manage. And then she got out, running toward the two sheriffs. Another lawman in the yard, a deputy, tried to stop her from getting closer, but she batted his hands away.

"My son is in there!"

"It's okay," Cooper assured the deputy. "Let her through."

Laurel didn't take the time to thank him or

to respond to the glare Jericho was giving her for disobeying his order. She rushed past the men and hurried into the house. The room was dark, only a corner lamp for illumination, so she needed a moment for her eyes to adjust and take everything in.

Some of the furniture and a Christmas tree had been toppled over. Things were strewn around. Evidence of the struggle that'd taken place here.

Then her heart bashed against her ribs.

Because she saw the blood. On the floor. And on the front of Sandy's white T-shirt.

"Oh, God." Laurel's gaze flew past her friend and to the medic.

Who was holding Maddox.

"He's all right," Sandy quickly told her. The medic repeated a variation of the same thing.

Laurel didn't believe either of them. She hurried to her son, praying there'd be no blood on him. There wasn't. She took him from the medic's arms, trying to check every inch of him. Maddox didn't cry, didn't seem upset, but he did look a little confused about what was going on.

"He wasn't hurt," Sandy insisted.

Laurel shook her head. "But the blood."

"It's mine." Sandy lifted the sleeve of her T-shirt, and Laurel saw the angry gash on her friend's arm.

That gave Laurel a new burst of emotions.

Concern and the sickening dread that she'd put her friend in danger. "I'm so sorry."

Sandy shrugged. "I just got grazed by a bullet, that's all. Nothing serious. The medic will stitch me up, but I wanted him to check out Maddox first."

"The kid's fine," the medic assured her. He goosed Maddox in the belly and went toward Sandy to start examining her.

"I can't ever thank you enough," Laurel told the woman.

"No thanks needed." Sandy's attention went to Jericho. "But I'd appreciate it if you caught the scum who did this."

Jericho nodded. "I will." And it sounded like a promise. One that Laurel hoped he could keep.

"Boo-boo," Maddox said, pointing to Sandy's arm.

Since Laurel didn't want him to see that, she sheltered his face against her shoulder and moved to the other part of the room.

And practically ran right into Jericho.

The moment seemed to freeze. Or maybe she felt that way because Laurel's feet suddenly seemed anchored in place. But then, Jericho didn't move, either. He just stood there, his attention fixed on Maddox.

Maddox gave him a wary look, his gaze sliding from Jericho's cowboy hat, face and finally to the shiny badge on his shirt. Maddox smiled.

Jericho sure didn't.

Laurel saw all the emotions go through his eyes. The love, instant and strong. The fear that he'd come so close to losing him. And finally the hatred. Not aimed at Maddox but at her.

For keeping Maddox from him.

"We need to leave," Jericho said to her. Not easily. His jaw muscles were as hard as granite.

Well, they were until Maddox smiled again.

Jericho's expression softened a bit. Then it softened a lot when he reached out and touched his son's cheek. That seemed to be the only invitation Maddox needed, because he reached for Jericho and that badge.

But Jericho didn't get a chance to take him.

Because Cooper stuck his head through the partially opened door. The lawman's attention went straight to Jericho. Then her. "My deputy caught one of them," Cooper said. "It's not good."

No. Laurel wasn't sure she could handle any more bad news tonight.

"What's wrong?" Jericho asked, walking closer to his fellow sheriff.

"I have to get all of you out of here now," Cooper insisted, glancing at both Jericho and Laurel.

"The kidnapper we caught told my deputy that more men were on the way here, and they have orders to shoot to kill."

Chapter Five

Shoot to kill.

Not exactly orders that Jericho had wanted to hear, but it'd gotten Laurel, Maddox and him hurrying away from the scene and to the sheriff's office in Appaloosa Pass. That wasn't exactly ideal for a toddler, but it would have to do until Jericho could make other arrangements.

And put an end to the danger.

The first would be a whole lot easier than the last.

Sandy didn't have any info about the kidnappers, and the one captured kidnapper was no longer talking, other than to tell them that those shoot-to-kill orders were meant only for Laurel and him. Jericho felt no relief about the fact that Maddox had been excluded in that hit plan because the baby could have easily been hurt in the attack.

Someone would pay for that.

Herschel, no doubt. But it was going to be a bear to prove his involvement.

Too bad Jax hadn't found the two gunmen in the black car who'd followed Jericho after the attack at his house. Jericho had indeed wounded at least one of them, because his brother had found blood on the road. But neither the car nor the men had been there by the time Jax arrived.

Not good.

He needed all these thugs in jail to up their chances of finding information to stop Herschel. Or anyone else who might be involved in this.

Jericho finished up his latest round of calls and made his way to the break room at the back of the building. Hardly living quarters, but there was a small bed that he and the deputies sometimes used when pulling double shifts. Tonight, however, Laurel and his son were sleeping in it.

It might take a while before those words—*his son*—didn't sound foreign to him. Not because of his feelings for the baby. No, he already loved the little boy. But his son was still a raw reminder that Laurel had kept Maddox from him.

Jericho didn't knock on the door because he didn't want to wake Laurel and the baby, but when he stepped inside the room, he saw that only Maddox was on the cot. The little boy was on his stomach, snuggled in some blankets. No snuggling for Laurel. She was pacing.

And crying.

Jericho saw that right off, though she did quickly wipe away the tears and turn from him. He shut the door so the noise from the squad room wouldn't disturb Maddox.

"Sandy just called," Laurel relayed before Jericho could say anything. "The doctor at the hospital checked her out and released her. She's on her way to Houston to stay with friends, and she told her parents not to come home until she's sure it's safe."

That was a smart move. The hired guns probably wouldn't go back to her place, but there was no sense taking that kind of risk, especially since they might see Sandy as a possible witness who needed to be eliminated. Jericho made a mental note to call Houston PD and arrange for some extra security for her.

"Please tell me the kidnapper you arrested is talking," she added. "And that he's got evidence to lead to my father's arrest."

"Afraid not." But she already knew that would be the answer. If he'd gotten big news like that, he would have come straight to her with it, and he darn sure wouldn't have been sporting a scowl.

A scowl that faded considerably when he went closer to his son.

Hard to scowl when looking at Maddox's face.

Jericho could see so much of himself in the boy. Some of Laurel, too.

"What about the other man?" she asked, walking to Jericho's side. "The one who tried to run you off the road. Is he talking?"

Jericho had to shake his head. "We know from his prints that his name is Travis DeWitt. He's got a record, a long one, but so far we haven't been able to connect him to your father."

"There's probably a connection." Laurel gave a heavy sigh and turned away from him again when she swiped at more tears.

She had plenty of reasons to cry. Someone had tried to kill her tonight, and that *someone* apparently wasn't giving up.

Part of him wanted to put his arm around her and try to comfort her. Thankfully, that part of him didn't win out, because the last thing he should do was have Laurel in his arms. Despite the bad blood, the attraction was still between them, too. No sense flaming that kind of heat when it would only make things more complicated than they already were.

She went to the table, picked up a notepad and handed it to him. "Those are the names of the people involved in the money laundering deal."

The deal that Herschel was using to try to have her arrested. There were only two names: Quinn Rossman and Diego Cawley.

"I've tried to dig up anything on them, of course," Laurel continued. "But so far, nothing. I thought it was just a simple real estate deal."

Because her father had no doubt wanted it to look that way.

"That's also the time line, as best as I can remember." She pointed to some dates, times and a brief description of phone conversations she'd had with Rossman and Cawley. "I didn't have any face-to-face meetings with either of them."

Jericho checked through the time line and saw that something was missing. "I'll need the exact dates of your mother's death and when you broke off your engagement." Because one or both of those could have triggered what was happening now.

While Laurel jotted down those dates, Jericho fired off a text to his brother Levi, who was a cop at the San Antonio Police Department, and asked him to run background checks on both men. Maybe Levi could dig up more than Laurel had. He also told his brother that he'd be faxing him a copy of the time line Laurel had just provided.

"So, what happens now?" she asked, handing him back the notepad.

Good question. But Jericho didn't have anything remotely resembling a good answer. "We keep looking for the idiots who attacked us. Keep looking for anything we can use to stop Herschel." He paused. "Please tell me you've got some dirt on him. Any kind of dirt that I can use to start legal proceedings for an arrest."

"No." Another heavy sigh. "Within minutes of Theo telling him that he wasn't Maddox's father and that I'd broken off the engagement, all my computer files and backups disappeared. They were corrupted by a virus that someone triggered."

That someone was no doubt one of Herschel's lackeys. "What about paper files?"

She shook her head. "All missing. By the time I got to my office, everything was gone."

Herschel had worked fast. But then, he'd probably had this backup plan ready to go for years just in case Laurel turned against him. Still, there was something about this that didn't make sense.

"You must have known your father would retaliate when you stopped being the perfect daughter."

"I did. But I didn't think he'd go this far." Her voice broke, and again Jericho had to stop himself from lending her a shoulder to cry on.

Hell.

He only managed to hold himself for a couple of seconds, and then, as if it had a mind of its own, his arm eased around her and pulled her closer. Until they were touching far more than they should. Of course, any kind of touching was out between Laurel and him. That didn't stop him.

Nope.

Jericho just waited until she wrestled with more of those tears. Thankfully, it didn't last long. But it was long enough for his body to get really stupid ideas about the touching.

"Sorry," Laurel said, and moved away from him.

Jericho got the feeling that the apology extended to a lot of things. Things he didn't want to get into right now since he was still seething over the fact that Laurel had kept his son from him. And all because she was afraid Herschel would have tried to kill him.

Which Herschel would have tried to do.

All the more reason to figure out how to put that idiot behind bars.

"I guess you didn't know Theo was going to tell your father the truth about Maddox when you broke off the engagement?" Jericho asked.

"I figured he would. Just not so soon." She pushed her hair from her face. "I wasn't thinking straight. My mother," Laurel added.

Yeah, he figured her grief for her mother had played into this. From all accounts, they'd been close.

"So, after your mother's death, you decided…

what?" Because Jericho was having a little trouble filling in the blanks. "That you didn't want to live by your father's dirty rules?"

Her gaze slowly came to his. "I think my father murdered my mother." No tears this time. There was a totally different emotion in her eyes and voice.

Anger.

And lots of it.

"You said she died from cancer," Jericho pointed out.

"I think he helped her death along with an overdose of pain meds." Laurel folded her arms over her chest. Started pacing again. "My mother wanted me to break off my engagement to Theo. She wanted me to leave and tell you the truth about Maddox."

Jericho didn't cheer out loud, but he was on her mother's side on this. "She was right."

"She was. And I think my father eavesdropped on our conversations and arranged for her to get an overdose of painkillers. Yes, she was sick. Very sick. But the chemo was working, and she wasn't so much out of it that she would have taken too big of a dose by accident. I think my father might have put them in her food or something."

That gave him a new surge of anger, too. Herschel preying on a sick woman because she wasn't toeing the line. "Was there an autopsy?"

"No. And my father had her cremated the same day she died."

Jericho wanted to curse. Hell. Now they were looking at murder. Two counts of it, since he was certain Herschel had also been responsible for his father's death.

"I was grieving," Laurel added, "and by the time I figured out what might have happened, it was already too late. Any evidence proving his guilt was cremated with my mother."

Which Jericho was betting wasn't an accident.

There was a soft knock on the door, and a moment later Jax opened it. "DeWitt's lawyer is here."

Good. Maybe the lawyer would convince his scummy client to talk.

Jax walked closer to them, and his gaze slid from Jericho to Laurel. Then to Maddox.

"He's your son." There wasn't a shred of doubt in Jax's voice. "How long have you known?"

"A couple of hours." That alone said plenty, but his brother deserved a whole lot more, especially since Jax knew the emotional wringer he'd been through over the years with Laurel and her father. "Herschel's trying to get custody."

Jax didn't look surprised, just as disgusted as Jericho was. "By trying to eliminate Laurel and you?"

"It looks that way. Herschel has dirt on Laurel to have her arrested." Jericho handed Jax the notepad with the time line and names. "I need that faxed to Levi so he can try to help with the threat of Laurel's arrest. But Herschel also has fake dirt to have her committed to the loony bin. Laurel wants me to marry her so she can transfer custody of Maddox to me."

His brother didn't say anything for several moments. "So, you'll marry her?"

That question just hung in the air, and before Jericho could even attempt an answer, he heard voices in the squad room. Loud ones.

"Wait here with Laurel," he told Jax, and Jericho drew his gun.

Bracing himself for another attack, Jericho hurried out of the break room and down the short hall to the squad room. But there was no attack. Their loud-talking visitors—a tall, bulky-shouldered man and a gray-haired woman—didn't appear to be armed. However, one of the deputies, Dexter, was frisking them, and neither seemed especially happy about that. The unhappiness went up a significant notch when the man's gaze landed on Jericho.

"Sheriff Crockett," he said like venom.

Jericho didn't recognize the guy, but venom like that was almost certainly personal.

"Theo James." Jericho put some venom in his voice, too.

"We want to see Laurel now," the woman demanded. And there was no doubt that it was a demand.

"And you are?" Jericho made sure he sounded like the sheriff when he asked that question.

"Dorothy James. Theo's mother."

Of course.

He didn't see much of a resemblance. Maybe because of the woman's slight build. She looked on the frail side, and her skin was as thin and white as paper. Unlike her son, who towered over her and had a tan despite it being the dead of winter.

Jericho knew that Theo James was a lawyer, like Laurel, but he could have passed for a bouncer. A well-dressed one, though. Jericho figured that suit had come with a big price tag. Ditto for the haircut. And it looked as if he'd had a manicure. As a general rule, he didn't trust men who had manicures.

Of course, he hadn't needed a manicure to feel that way about Theo James.

And Jericho was certain that jealousy wasn't playing into this.

Almost certain, anyway.

"Why do you want to see Laurel?" Jericho pressed.

Dorothy wasn't the sort of woman to hide her emotions. She huffed, glared and generally looked ready to run right over him to get to Laurel. "We heard about the attack, and I want to make sure she's okay. She's my son's fiancée."

"Ex-fiancée," Jericho corrected.

Oh, that did not please either Theo or his mom.

"The breakup is all just a misunderstanding," Theo answered. "And a temporary one. Once I speak with Laurel, we can sort it all out—"

"I doubt that. What do you know about the attack?"

"I don't like your tone," Dorothy snapped. "Are you implying we had something to do with it?"

Jericho stared at her. "Did you?"

"No!"

Man, the woman could yell, and all in the same breath, she belted out a denial and a threat to slap him with a defamation-of-character lawsuit. However, Theo wasn't denying much. That's because he had his attention nailed to the hall. More specifically, to the doorway of the break room where Laurel was standing.

"Laurel," Theo said on a rise of breath, and he started toward her.

He didn't get far because Jericho latched onto his arm. Yeah, the guy was big. Strong, too. But Jericho shoved him back.

"Stay put," Jericho warned him.

"Theo just wants to go to his fiancée." Dorothy

again. The woman turned her attention to Laurel. "Are you going to come out here and stop this asinine interrogation of the man you love?"

"No. She's not." And Jericho gave Laurel a warning glance. She didn't say anything, but she also didn't stay put. Not exactly a compromise since he didn't want Laurel in the same general area as the pair.

"Laurel, we need to talk," Theo said. He threw off Jericho's grip but didn't go closer. *"Alone."*

"Then talk. But it won't be alone," Laurel added. "Whatever you have to say, you say here."

Laurel took the words right out of Jericho's mouth. Except he'd intended to glare more than she had. Theo sure added some glare and snarl though—he aimed it at Jericho—before turning back to Laurel.

"Certainly you must know by now that calling off the engagement was a mistake," Theo said to her. "You've upset your father. Us. And yourself."

"Upset?" Laurel threw her hands in the air. "Gunmen attacked Jericho and me. That's why I'm upset." She walked toward them. "If you know anything about those gunmen, tell us."

"Of course we don't know anything," Dorothy insisted. "Now, get Maddox and come home with us. We'll make sure you're both safe." The woman paused. "Where is Maddox, anyway?"

"He's already safe," Jericho assured her.

Partly true. Jax was back there with Maddox, and a gunman would have to break into the back exit or come through the front to get to them. Still, Jericho wasn't about to share that with these two.

A staring match started between Theo and him. Dorothy joined in on it, but Jericho pretty much ignored her and focused on Laurel's ex.

"You think Theo here could be in on the attacks?" Jericho asked Laurel. He knew the question would rile mother and son. And it did.

Dorothy made a sound of pure outrage. "Theo had nothing to do with this. He loves Laurel. He only wants to marry her and be a father to Maddox."

"Maddox already has a father." Laurel's voice was hardly more than a whisper, but it was obvious Dorothy heard it loud and clear. She jerked back as if Laurel had slapped her.

"It's true," Theo said, his voice quiet, as well. "We'll discuss it later, Mom."

Okay, so Dorothy didn't know about Maddox's paternity, but like Jax, she had no trouble putting two and two together. Except in Dorothy's case, there was more disapproval than Jax had shown.

A lot more.

"Later," Theo warned his mother when it appeared she was ready to launch herself at Jericho.

He gently took hold of his mother's arm. "Laurel's tired and upset," he repeated, as if making a point. "I can talk to her in the morning when her head is clearer."

Jericho tapped his badge, pulling the lawman card, and he put his gun back in his holster. "You'll talk to me. And not in the morning. You'll do it right now. Is Herschel behind the attacks?"

"Of course," Dorothy answered without hesitation. "Who else?"

Jericho was thinking the *who else* could apply to the woman asking the question. And her hulk of a son. "If you disapprove of her father so much, then why insist Laurel marry Theo?" he asked.

Dorothy gave him an isn't-it-obvious? huff. "Because they're right for each other, that's why. And besides, even if Theo isn't Maddox's biological father, he's been a father to him. He deserves to raise that little boy."

"Theo's hardly seen Maddox." Laurel went to Jericho's side, stared at Dorothy. "For that matter, Theo's hardly seen me over the past six months."

Six months? The more Jericho learned about this unholy union, the less he liked it. Soon, very soon, he'd want to know why Laurel had gotten involved with the guy in the first place.

"Theo hasn't seen Maddox or you much

because he's been working out of state, that's why. And I'm betting Theo's seen more of Maddox than his so-called birth father has." With that zinger, Dorothy added a smug nod. No doubt to rile Jericho.

It worked.

However, Jericho reined in his temper so he could try to get some usable info from these two clowns. Except he realized it would have to wait a second or two when he heard footsteps. They weren't coming from the break room but rather from the side hall where the holding cell was located. The man who appeared was wearing a pricey suit like Theo's.

DeWitt's attorney, no doubt.

"Did you get your client to talk?" Jericho asked him.

The lawyer didn't introduce himself, didn't even spare Jericho a glance. "I've advised him to remain silent. If he's smart, he'll listen." He went past Dexter and let himself out. He shut the door so hard that it shook the nearby Christmas tree and sent the sparse ornaments jangling.

A moment later, Mack, the other deputy, came out from the holding-cell area. "DeWitt's all locked up." He volleyed his attention between Theo and his mother. "Want me to arrest somebody?"

"Not yet. Maybe soon." Jericho turned back

to Theo. "Okay, I'll bite. If you know Maddox isn't yours, then why would you want to marry Laurel?"

Theo looked at Jericho as if he'd sprouted horns. "Because I love Maddox and her, that's why."

Maybe. But something about this felt as wrong as wrong could feel. "I don't know all of what's going on, but I suspect there's either money or power involved. Money and power you'll lose somehow if you don't have your ring on Laurel's finger."

Bingo.

Dorothy got some fire in her dust-gray eyes. Theo's teeth came together for a moment. Neither of them, however, jumped to volunteer anything.

However, Laurel did. "Theo and my father were involved in several business deals. Major ones. And some of the investors pulled out when I broke off the engagement."

All right. Now, *that* was motive.

"How big were these business deals?" Jericho asked.

"Millions," Laurel provided.

Yeah, definitely motive.

"A misunderstanding, that's all," Theo insisted. "A few of the investors were worried that I didn't have Herschel's backing. I do. And once that's made clear, then they'll pony up the money again."

"So, you've got Herschel's backing even if he's trying to murder the woman you want to marry?" Jericho concluded.

"My mother accused Herschel of wrongdoing. You didn't hear that from me. And you won't," Theo added. "Because I don't believe Herschel would do anything like this."

Interesting. Dorothy's reaction was interesting, as well. She turned those frosty eyes on her son.

"If Herschel's not behind this, then who is?" Jericho asked Theo.

"You and your family maybe," Theo answered. "From everything I've heard, none of your siblings or your mother wants you involved with Laurel."

They didn't. But Jericho had no intention of admitting that to this beefed-up jerk. He tapped his badge again. "I'm a lawman. My brothers are all lawmen, too. That means we're not into attempted murder or other assorted felonies. Now, talk. If not Herschel, then who? And this time, I want your answer to make sense."

Theo's mouth tightened. "You'd have to ask Laurel. I suspect she was involved with someone else, or she wouldn't have ended our engagement. Someone who's angry enough to want her dead."

Laurel cursed, something he'd rarely heard her do over the years. "There was no one else."

"Right." Theo shot Jericho a glare.

"It appears you've got something to say to me?" Jericho challenged.

Oh, Theo wanted to say plenty, all right, but Jericho saw the moment the man reined in his manicured claws.

Dorothy, however, appeared to be sharpening hers. "When you look at other suspects, look at a businessman named Quinn Rossman."

The very man involved in the money laundering scheme that Herschel was trying to use to have Laurel arrested. Theo clearly knew the name, too. Clearly didn't like his mother mentioning it, because he glared at her.

A glare that the woman ignored. "Rossman's the one who'll take the biggest financial loss because of these failed deals," Dorothy added.

So, the claws weren't for Jericho but for this Quinn Rossman.

Laurel nodded. "Quinn Rossman will lose several of those millions, but like everyone else involved in this, I haven't found anything to link him to what's going on with the attacks."

"Then, keep looking," Dorothy insisted. "You don't have to worry about his moron of a partner, Diego Cawley. He doesn't have the stones or the brains to do something like this."

"Mom," Theo whispered. And it was indeed a warning. "You've said enough."

Jericho didn't agree. He wanted to hear a whole lot more. "You seem to know plenty about these two, Rossman and Cawley. How much do you know about their money laundering deal?" He stared at Dorothy, waiting for an answer.

"She knows nothing about that," Theo snapped, and he took his mother's arm. "If you want to question us further, then contact our attorney." He rattled off his lawyer's name and left, practically dragging his mother with him.

"Want me to stop them?" Mack asked.

Jericho gave it some thought, and while it would give him some instant gratification to grill Theo like a common criminal, he wasn't likely to get any other answers from the pair. Not tonight, anyway.

"No, let them go," he told Mack before turning to Laurel. "You need to be back in the break room. Away from these windows." They were bullet resistant and the blinds were pulled all the way down, but there was no sense taking any chances.

Laurel motioned toward the break room. "What about the door that's in there?"

"It leads to the parking lot, and it's reinforced and locked. Wired to the security system, too. If anyone tries to come in that way or through the windows, the alarm will sound."

Apparently satisfied with that, she nodded. However, Jericho and Laurel had only made it a few steps when he heard a thudding sound coming from the other side of the building.

From the holding cell.

Both deputies went running in that direction. Jericho nearly followed them but instead decided it was wise to move Laurel into his office just off the hall. There was a single window in there, but it stayed locked. It was also bullet resistant and wired to the security system.

"What's going on?" Jericho called out to the deputies.

No answer. But he could hear them moving around and cursing. What had gone wrong now?

"Wait here," he ordered Laurel.

With his gun drawn, Jericho hurried to the other hall, and he didn't have to go far before he saw the deputies in the holding cell. His first thought was that DeWitt was trying to escape.

But he wasn't. DeWitt was sprawled on the floor.

Dead.

Chapter Six

Laurel opened her eyes and nearly bolted from the bed. It took her a moment to realize where she was.

In the guest room at the Appaloosa Pass Ranch that the Crocketts owned.

Not Jericho's place, either, but the main house. Where most of his family still lived. The same family who despised her. And they had reasons for hating her. Her father's possible involvement with Sherman Crockett's murder, and now she'd kept Jericho in the dark about Maddox.

Her being here would only rub salt in a still-open wound.

Along with possibly bringing the danger to their doorstep. The danger was still there because they didn't have the answers to stop it. Answers they definitely wouldn't get from DeWitt, the man who'd rammed into Jericho's truck.

That's because DeWitt had committed suicide. The cause of death was a dose of poison that his lawyer had likely slipped him. Of course, last she'd heard, the lawyer was nowhere to be found. The man could have been another hired killer like the ones who were already after her.

Yet, Jericho had insisted on bringing Maddox and her here to the ranch. Despite her objections. He'd said they could discuss it after a good night's sleep and by then she would see that this was the right move.

Well, it was morning, the sunlight seeping through the edges of the blinds, and Laurel still wasn't convinced coming here had been the right thing to do.

Easing out of the bed, she glanced down at the borrowed T-shirt she'd used as a gown. Maybe Jericho's. But thankfully, it didn't carry his scent. She already had too many reminders of the man without having that.

She checked on Maddox, who was still asleep in the crib in the corner of the room. Thankfully, Jericho hadn't had to go to any trouble to find the crib. It was already set up because Jax's fifteen-month-old son sometimes stayed over. Also thankfully, Maddox had slept through the night. Probably because he'd been as exhausted by their ordeal as she'd been.

Laurel looked at the clock on the nightstand, almost seven, and she hurried to the adjoining bathroom so she could grab a shower. Even though the steamy water felt heavenly on her tight muscles, she stayed in the shower only a couple of minutes because Maddox would be up soon. Someone—Jericho's mother, Iris, or maybe the housekeeper—had left her clean underwear and toiletries.

Since she hadn't gotten any clothes from her house, Laurel was forced to put back on the jeans and red sweater she'd worn the night before when she had gone to Jericho's house to ask him to marry her. Clearly, that plan hadn't worked.

Nothing had.

She'd need a change of clothes soon. And a change of location. That meant hiring body-guards and moving Maddox to some kind of safe house. No way could she stay at the Crocketts' ranch another night.

Laurel hurried back into the bedroom and practically skidded to a halt when she spotted Jericho. She hadn't heard anything to indicate he was in the guest room. But there he was.

Holding Maddox.

"I didn't hear him wake up," she said. "I didn't hear *you*."

Jericho looked up at her, a half smile on his face, but the smile vanished as quickly as it'd come, and he made a manly sounding grunt. It took Laurel a moment to realize that had some-thing to do with the fact that she was still pulling down her sweater. She hadn't exactly flashed him, but since her bra was nothing but flimsy white lace, he'd gotten an eyeful. She quickly fixed that.

"I heard Maddox and came in to check on him." Jericho turned his attention back to the baby.

"He was fussing?" She wanted to kick herself for not hearing it. And for taking a shower. And for the bra peep show.

"Not exactly. He was just moving around in the crib. I tapped on the door, and when you didn't answer, I came in to make sure he was okay."

Well, Maddox certainly wasn't fussing now. Jericho had taken off his badge, and Maddox was playing with it. Smiling, too. And yes, it was the same half smile that she'd just seen on Jericho's face.

She went to them, expecting Maddox to reach for her, but her son clearly was more interested in the badge and the man holding him.

"Tar," Maddox babbled. His attempt at saying star—the shape of the badge. Something that Jericho had obviously already taught him. But that wasn't all Jericho had done.

"You changed his diaper?" she asked when she saw the fresh one Maddox was wearing.

Jericho nodded. "He'd stripped off the other one. When I came in, he was bare-butt naked."

Not unusual. Maddox often did that. In fact, she was surprised he still had on the cotton T-shirt, since he'd recently learned to pull that off, as well.

"Anyway, I found the diaper bag and put a fresh one on him," Jericho finished.

It was as if she'd stepped into an alternate universe. "You know how to change a diaper?"

Maybe her tone was a little insulting, because she got a flash of a scowl. "Jax is a dad. We've all had some practice."

"Of course." In fact, since Jax was a widower and worked both at the sheriff's office and the ranch, he and his son probably spent a lot of time here.

But not now.

She'd heard Jericho say the nanny had taken Jax's little boy to relatives who lived out of the county. Wise move, considering it wasn't safe to be around her. Still, it meant Jax wasn't with his son right now, and with Christmas so close, she figured Jax wasn't happy about that.

She certainly wasn't.

"How is Jax?" she asked. "I mean, since his wife died." And not just died. His wife, Paige, had been murdered by a vicious serial killer called the Moonlight Strangler, who'd been murdering women for over three decades.

"Jax's dealing as best he can." As if it was the most natural thing in the world, Jericho took a pair of overalls from the diaper bag and put them on Maddox. "It'd help if we could catch the bastard who killed her. Well, it'd help Jax to better deal with her murder, anyway."

What Jericho wasn't saying was that the Moonlight Strangler had more than one emotional hold on his family. The killer was also the biological father of Jericho's adopted sister, Addie. So, yes, catching the Moonlight Strangler would give Jax and plenty of other families some much-needed justice, but if and when that happened, it wouldn't be easy for Addie to have to deal with the man who'd fathered her.

Of course, other than Jax's wife, the Moonlight Strangler had left Addie and her adopted family alone. And even more, it was rumored that the serial killer had developed an eerie attachment to the Crocketts and had even helped them solve a recent case where Addie had been in danger.

"Jax's son is much too young to remember his mom," Jericho added a moment later. "I guess that's both good and bad. He doesn't remember she was killed. And it helps that Jax has family to step in and try to fill the void."

"You've stepped in," she pointed out. "I just hadn't expected you to be a hands-on kind of uncle."

All right, that earned her another scowl. She was batting a thousand in the piss-off-Jericho-this-morning department.

But then Jericho shrugged and smiled when Maddox looked up at him. "Guess that means you didn't expect me to be a hands-on kind of father, either. Well, expect it because that's exactly what I'll be."

That sounded like a threat. And it probably was. Laurel hadn't thought for one second that she could tell Jericho about Maddox and that he'd then quietly step away.

Jericho wasn't the *quietly* type.

But she also hadn't expected to feel, well, *this*. Maybe a little jealousy. Was that it? Apparently so. For eighteen months, it'd just been mainly Maddox, her mother and her. Theo and her father had rarely been in the picture. Laurel hadn't braced herself nearly enough to share Maddox with his own father.

Nor had she braced herself for being so close to Jericho again.

She'd thought that over two years would be enough to make herself immune to him. No such luck.

"There should be a vaccination that women

can take for when they're around men like you." She hadn't intended to say that aloud. It just slipped out. And she thought maybe Jericho would be puzzled by it.

But no.

She got that brief half smile again. The one that turned her brain to mush and made her feel like a hormone-raged, sixteen-year-old girl again.

The heat came. Of course it did. Sliding through her. Jericho dropped his gaze to her mouth, and even though there were still several inches of space between them, she could have sworn she felt him kiss her.

"Yeah," Jericho said. He didn't look any happier about this heat than she was. But he looked just as affected.

Good grief.

Laurel shook her head to clear it. "I'll need to make other arrangements for a place to stay."

"Already in the works. But I figure we'll be okay here for a while."

She didn't like the sound of that. "How long is awhile?"

Jericho's forehead bunched up. "As long as it takes. Maddox's safety has to come first, agreed?"

Laurel nodded, but her agreement was just for the Maddox-coming-first part of that. "As long as it takes?" she repeated. "Because you know I can't stay here. Your family—"

"Won't be a problem. They know I'm Maddox's father. I told all of them."

All of them, meaning his mother, three brothers, his sister and her fiancé. Laurel had expected it, of course. News like that wouldn't stay secret for long, especially since Jericho was close to his family.

"They'll hate me now even more for keeping Maddox from you all these months," she said on a heavy sigh.

"Well, it didn't earn you any gold stars." He tipped his head to her face. At least, she thought it was her face. She realized he was actually looking at her mouth. "That won't, either."

"That?" Again, it was something she shouldn't have asked out loud. No need to clarify anything when it came to her mouth and his.

"That," he verified, and touched her lips with his index finger. Like the previous look, it felt very much like a kiss. "We're good together like *that*, but it's the only way we're good together. My family knows it, and they won't want me tangled up with you again."

It was true. They were good together when kissing. And in bed. But they couldn't live in bed forever, and the real world always came crashing in. After all, she'd always be Herschel's daughter, and in the eyes of his family, she would always be the one who helped her father get away with murder.

Too bad it was partly true.

If she'd just figured out a way to stop him. Or at least have found some evidence that would lead to his arrest. But nothing.

"Don't worry," Jericho added. "No one will object to you being here."

Only because of Maddox. And it made her wonder—would the Crocketts soon want her out of the picture?

Probably.

That wouldn't happen. Despite the mess she'd made of her life, Maddox was her son, and even though he had Crockett blood, she wouldn't just let Jericho push her out of their son's life.

"I'm bringing in your father for questioning this morning," Jericho tossed out there.

That got her attention. "You talked to him?"

He shook his head. "Only spoke to one of his lawyers and told him if Herschel didn't come in, that I'd put out a warrant for his arrest."

Her gut twisted. Not because her father shouldn't be questioned. He should be. But an ultimatum like that was like poking a stick at a bed of rattlers.

"Maddox and you will stay here while I talk to him," Jericho went on. Not really a request. More of an order. "Chase and Levi will be coming to the ranch, to make sure you're safe."

"But what about you? Someone tried to kill you, too."

He tapped his badge. "That goes with the territory."

As arguments went, that one sucked. Because she was the reason he was in this *territory*.

"Talking to my father won't help," she reminded him. "In fact, prepare yourself because he'll probably have some out-of-county lawman with him who'll insist on you turning me over to him so I can be arrested or locked up in a mental hospital."

"Yeah, I figure he'll try to pull something like that. But I've got three hours before the meeting, and I'm hoping between now and then we can find something to connect him to the hired guns who've been coming after us."

"Good luck with that." Sarcasm aside, she meant it. And then she had a thought. "Maybe while you're with my father, I can somehow get into his office and find something. Not just connected to this, but also to your father's murder. My mother's death, too."

Jericho didn't shake his head. He just gave her a flat look to let her know that wasn't going to happen. "Just in case he's the one who wants you dead, let's not make it easy for him."

"Just in case?" she repeated. "You're thinking maybe it's not him, after all?"

"I'm thinking there are other suspects. Theo and his Mommy Dearest. Diego Cawley and Quinn Rossman. And no, adding Theo to the suspect list doesn't have anything to do with the fact that he's your ex-lover."

"My ex-fiancé, not my lover," she corrected without thinking.

She should have thought first.

Because Jericho honed right in on that. "Something you want to tell me, Laurel?"

"No." And she was certain of that. Best not to get into why she'd allowed herself to accept a proposal from Theo. Jericho already thought too little of her, and that wouldn't help.

Besides, it wasn't any of his business.

Though Jericho's look said differently. Still, he didn't press it, thank goodness. "Levi called earlier about those two men, Rossman and Cawley, who were involved in the money laundering deal."

"And?" she couldn't ask fast enough.

"Lots of shady deals but no arrests. Also, just as you said, there's no obvious link to your father. *Obvious*," Jericho repeated. "But one of Rossman and Cawley's companies did business with Theo's mother. And I'm not talking about the deal your father's trying to use to put you in jail. This was something that happened well over a year ago."

"How'd Levi find that?"

"Apparently, the FBI had Rossman and Cawley under surveillance for a while. Nothing turned up, but the agent kept track of all the men's contacts. Dorothy was one of them. So were you." Jericho paused. "Who did the initial paperwork for the money laundering deal?"

She huffed. "My father, of course."

"So, there had to have been some kind of communication between him and Rossman and Cawley. I'll have Levi keep digging."

It was a long shot, but maybe, just maybe, something would finally turn up.

"Maddox will be hungry soon," she said, forcing the conversation in a different direction. "He doesn't take a bottle, but he'll need cereal or something."

"I'm pretty sure Ellie and Mom will be fixing some oatmeal," Jericho finally said, a muscle flickering in his jaw.

Ellie, their longtime housekeeper. She probably wouldn't care for Laurel being there, either.

"I can't make this perfect for you," Jericho said as if reading her mind. With Maddox still in his arms, he headed toward the door and the stairs.

Laurel followed after them. "At least tell

me someone found the kidnapper and he's been arrested."

"Afraid not." Jericho glanced back at her. No heat this time. Just the same worry she figured was in her own eyes. "Not yet, anyway. But Jax and the other deputies are working on it."

Jericho likely had been, too. There was more than worry and brief flashes of forbidden heat for her in those amber eyes. There was also plenty of exhaustion, which probably meant he'd been up most of the night—something she should have done, as well. But the adrenaline crash had gotten the best of her and, despite the nightmares, Laurel had gotten some sleep.

He led her through the family room, and the Christmas tree with the twinkling lights instantly caught Maddox's attention.

"Pretty," he said. Or rather he said a baby version of the word. And he repeated it with each new decoration. The wreaths on the walls and the gold angels and a trio of stuffed Santas on the mantel.

"My mom really gets into Christmas," Jericho said as they passed another decorated tree in the hall. There was yet another small one in the eating area just off the kitchen.

Normally, Laurel made a big deal out of the holidays, too, but with grieving over her mother's death and trying to escape her father, the holidays hadn't exactly been in the forefront of her thoughts. Too bad, because Maddox deserved Christmas. Instead, they'd dodged bullets.

And she would have to dodge more. Not literal ones this time. But rather, Jericho's mother. Iris was at the stove, stirring a pot of oatmeal. She looked up, sparing Laurel a frosty glance, but her expression warmed considerably when she spotted Maddox.

"There he is." Smiling, Iris put aside the wooden spoon, and wiping her hands on her apron, she walked toward them. She held out her arms, and Laurel got yet another surprise when Maddox went to her.

Maddox had *met* his grandmother hours earlier when they had first arrived at the ranch house, but Maddox hadn't been fully awake then. And Iris hadn't exactly been in a chatty mood, especially since she'd just learned that Jericho was Maddox's father. Laurel was certain Jericho had gotten an earful about that after Laurel had gone to bed.

"He's usually a little shy around strangers," Laurel remarked. Obviously, though, he didn't consider Iris a stranger. Or the enemy.

Unlike the way Iris felt about her.

After a few snuggles with Maddox, Iris finally made eye contact with her. "I can't forget that my husband is dead. Murdered. And it's all because of your family. You might not have pulled the trigger, but you also didn't help us put Herschel behind bars. Now it's led to this."

Laurel nodded, was about to assure her that she couldn't forget it, either, but Iris continued before she could say anything.

"But we need a truce," Iris said. "Certainly not for your sake but for Maddox's. Agreed?"

"Agreed." It definitely wasn't a warm fuzzy welcome, but then Laurel hadn't expected one.

Iris's smile returned. Aimed at Maddox, of course. "Are you hungry, sweetie?" Iris asked him. "Because Grandma and Ellie made some oatmeal. Scrambled eggs, too."

Laurel noticed the easy way *Grandma* had rolled off her tongue. It had to be hard because of the bad blood between their families. Still, Iris was either putting on a good show or else she wasn't letting any of that bad blood extend to Maddox.

"The oatmeal will be fine." Laurel went to the stove to dish him up a bowl so it could cool.

"Tar," Maddox said, showing Iris Jericho's badge.

"Yes, it is. A pretty one. And there's another star. A gold one." Iris pointed to the one on top of the Christmas tree by the breakfast table, and she went in that direction with Maddox. Maddox discarded the badge when Iris plucked off a horse ornament for him to play with.

That's when Laurel noticed the blinds were down. Not just in the breakfast area, either, but in the kitchen, as well. That probably wasn't their usual position, but she was thankful for it. The ranch was likely well protected, but that didn't mean someone with a rifle couldn't fire a shot into the house, as they'd done to Jericho's the night before.

Not exactly a good thought to settle her already churning stomach.

And speaking of unsettling things, Laurel glanced around at the empty kitchen. She'd known Chase and Levi wouldn't be there yet, but she'd expected to see the others. "Where is everyone?"

Iris and Jericho exchanged an uneasy glance before Jericho answered. "Addie and Weston are in Austin visiting his sister. Jax's son is staying with his other grandmother for a few days."

Laurel understood the uneasy glance then. "They're not here because of me. Because of the danger." She huffed. "Maddox and I should have been the ones to stay elsewhere."

"Nonsense." Iris got another ornament off the tree for Maddox. "Addie and Weston understand."

Laurel didn't get a chance to argue about

that because Jericho's phone rang, and she saw Jax's name on the screen. Since this probably had something to do with the investigation, he stepped out of the breakfast area and into the hall.

"I'll feed Maddox," Iris volunteered, taking the bowl of oatmeal from Laurel.

"Thank you." And Laurel meant it. She was thankful because it gave her the opportunity to go into the hall with Jericho and listen in on his conversation.

Jericho didn't put the call on speaker. Probably because he didn't want his mother to hear if it turned out to be more bad news. That meant Laurel had to go close to him.

Very close.

And despite the fact her mind should be on anything but Jericho, her body gave her a little nudge to let her know Jericho would always be on her mind.

"We haven't found anything on DeWitt's lawyer," she heard Jax say. "He used a fake ID when he checked into the sheriff's office, and we can't get any usable fingerprints off the sign-in sheet."

All planned, no doubt. Heck, the man probably wasn't even a lawyer.

"I reviewed the surveillance footage from the camera outside the holding cell," Jax continued, "and he did hand DeWitt some papers. It's possible that's when he passed DeWitt the poison he used to kill himself."

"So, he didn't actually murder him," Jericho concluded. "Any reason why DeWitt would commit suicide?"

"Nothing I can find so far." Jax added something under his breath she didn't catch. Profanity, maybe. "In fact, I'm not finding anything on anybody that'll put an end to this danger."

Jericho whispered some of that profanity himself. "Get some rest. I'll be there in about an hour."

He pushed the button to end the call but didn't budge. Maybe because Jericho needed a moment to take some of the gloom and doom off his face. Laurel was sure there was plenty of it on her face, as well.

"What now?" she asked.

Jericho stared at her and touched her arm, rubbed gently. "I'll make arrangements for a safe house for the three of us."

She was partly relieved that Jericho would be going with her. No one would protect Maddox the way he would. But Laurel reminded herself that being under the same roof with Jericho just wasn't a good idea.

Jericho must have gotten that same jolting reminder because he glanced down at where he was rubbing her arm and eased back his hand. He looked ready to apologize.

Or kiss her.

That stupid part of Laurel was hoping for the kiss. But he didn't get a chance to do either because the phone in the kitchen rang. Jericho hurried to answer it, but his mother beat him to it.

"Teddy," Iris greeted. She was still holding Maddox in her arms. Still smiling, but the smile quickly faded. "I'll let Jericho know."

"Teddy's a ranch hand," Jericho explained to Laurel. "What'd he want?" he asked his mother the moment she hung up.

"We have a visitor," Iris said, her voice practically trembling. "Herschel Tate just arrived, and he's demanding to see his daughter."

Chapter Seven

Hell. This was not the way Jericho had wanted to start the morning. Yes, he'd braced himself to interrogate Herschel. But not now and not here at the ranch.

And definitely not with Laurel and Maddox around.

"Oh, God," Laurel said under her breath.

He hated that her father could put that kind of fear on her face. Hated even more that the fear was warranted.

Jericho took the phone from his mother, but for Maddox's sake, he tried to appear calm. He figured he was failing, but maybe Maddox wouldn't be as frightened as Laurel was.

"Teddy," Jericho greeted the ranch hand, and he put the call on speaker so Laurel could hear. His mother moved into the hall with Maddox. "Where's our visitor now?"

"Herschel's still in his car in the driveway.

I've got a gun pointed at him. That was the right thing to do, wasn't it?"

"Absolutely." Jericho had instructed all the hands to keep an eye out for a possible attack, and this could be the start of one. Of course, it'd be pretty stupid of Herschel to come to the ranch and personally try to attack them. "Keep the gun on him. Is he alone?"

"No. There's a woman and another fella with him. And a driver. The woman says her name is Nan Winston, Herschel's lawyer, and the fella introduced himself as Laurel's fiancé."

Laurel groaned. "Ex-fiancé. And what the heck is Theo doing here? Why are any of them here?"

Both good questions, but Jericho doubted their visitors would provide the answers to Teddy.

"I want to see my daughter," he heard Herschel insist. Not exactly a shout but close enough.

With Herschel's temper and mean streak, the man might provoke Teddy into a fight just so he could shoot the ranch hand. Of course, Teddy knew how to handle a gun. That's why Jericho had posted him out front. Still, it was best if Jericho went outside and faced down this idiot and his entourage. Besides, he might even get Herschel to say something incriminating so he could arrest him.

Or so Jericho could shoot him.

It was probably wrong to wish that, but after the things Herschel had done, he deserved a bullet or two.

"Wait inside," Jericho told Laurel. "And I mean it. I don't want your father to even know you and Maddox are here."

Laurel suddenly no longer looked afraid, and she darn sure wasn't trembling. "He already knows or he wouldn't have shown up. I need to stand up to him."

"Admirable. But it's not the right time."

She shook her head, no doubt ready to launch into an argument. One that Jericho intended to nip in the bud. He took hold of her arm and moved her deeper into the kitchen so Maddox wouldn't hear. Maddox probably wouldn't be able to understand what was being said, but Jericho didn't want to risk it.

"Both the so-called lawyer and driver could be armed," Jericho reminded her. "Plus, you don't need to go another round with delusion-boy Theo. At best, he has a serious issue with reality by still referring to himself as your fiancé. At worst, he wants you dead and is trying to goad you into coming out."

Her chin stayed firm. "I need to stand up to him, too."

"Again, admirable. But it's not going to happen. Not until one or both of them are behind bars."

Jericho took his badge from the table and clipped it on. He was already wearing his holster and weapon, something he normally didn't do around the house, but then just about everything that'd happened in the past twenty-four hours had been far from normal.

"They could gun you down, too," Laurel said, following him to the front.

Jericho took hold of her. There were sidelight windows on both sides of the door, and while there was holly and such rimming the glass, he didn't want to risk Herschel's seeing her. Jericho glanced out, though, and saw not only Teddy but three other ranch hands.

All armed.

Their visitors were still inside the car. Or rather the limo. But the left-side passenger's door was open.

"I'll be okay." Jericho put on his jacket and Stetson. "And remember that part about staying inside." He shot her a warning glance he hoped would do the trick and make her stay put.

He didn't open the front door until he made sure Laurel wouldn't be in anyone's line of sight, and he went onto the porch, closing the door behind him. It was cold, and he got a full blast of that cold when the wind battered into him. The temperature was yet another reason to end this conversation fast so he could get Herschel and the others off the ranch.

The moment Jericho went down the stairs, someone stepped out of the limo. Herschel. He'd always been a big man, and he still was, even in his late sixties. Not overweight, just bulky. He'd always looked formidable to Jericho.

That hadn't changed, either.

He, too, was wearing a cowboy hat and a heavy jacket. Jericho didn't care much for that jacket because it could conceal a weapon.

"What the hell do you want, Herschel?" Jericho didn't want to sound even marginally pleasant.

His question must have spurred the others into action, because Theo stepped out, and he was soon followed by a leggy blonde wearing a red dress. Hardly the right garb for butt-freezing weather. This was no doubt Nan Winston, Herschel's lawyer.

"You know what I want—to see my daughter. Tell her to come out."

Jericho would take a hit with a hot branding iron first. "Who says she's here?"

Herschel jammed his thumb against his chest. "I do. My daughter's predicable."

He made a sound to let Herschel know he didn't agree with that. Laurel was far from predicable.

"Tell your driver, aka thug, to get out of the car, too," Jericho ordered. "I expect this little chat to be short and sweet. Emphasis on the short part. But I want everyone to keep their hands where I can see them."

Herschel chuckled, obviously trying to dismiss any danger that Jericho might pose to them. "You're going to shoot us, *Sheriff*?"

"Maybe. Haven't had my coffee yet, and I'm a bit testy. My advice—don't test me anymore. Do as I've said, speak your piece and then get the hell out of here."

No more chuckling, but his words did spur some glares from the trio. The driver also stepped out. He didn't lift his hands in the air, but he did put them on the car door in plain sight.

"I know my daughter's here," Herschel argued. "I had someone watching the sheriff's office, and they called and said you brought her and Maddox to your family's ranch. I gotta say, that wasn't very predictable."

Jericho shrugged, not fessing up to anything.

But Jericho had to admit to himself that it was possible for someone to have followed him from the sheriff's office. Not all the way to the ranch however. Even though he'd been bone tired, he would have noticed another vehicle on the rural road, but Herschel's hired morons could have seen the route he was taking and figured out he was going to the ranch.

"I'm here to take my daughter and grandson home," Herschel insisted.

"Really?" Jericho challenged "You honestly think I'd let that happen?"

"The law's on my side, Jericho. I have proof Laurel's not mentally fit to be a mother."

"Says you."

"And a team of respected psychiatrists," Herschel countered.

"Which you bought and paid for," Jericho countered right back.

Herschel didn't deny it. "She got involved with you and got pregnant. That proves she's not stable."

"No." Jericho stretched that out a few syllables. "It proves she was once attracted to me, that's all."

Oh, Herschel didn't like that one bit. Herschel really wouldn't like it if Jericho pointed out that the attraction was still there. Jericho certainly wasn't pleased about it, either.

"Laurel committed a crime," Herschel tried again.

"That's the pot calling the kettle black. Or did you think I'd forget all about you ordering my father's murder?"

Now Herschel got a smug look. So did the

skinny lawyer. "But there's proof of Laurel's crime," the lawyer said. "No proof whatsoever of Herschel's wrongdoing. Unlike his daughter, he has a spotless record."

No smug look for Jericho. He huffed, and because he really was testy, he put his hand over his gun. "You know, I'm getting a little tired of you bantering around this so-called proof you have against Laurel. Where is it?"

"You'll see it soon." Herschel checked his watch. "The warrant for her arrest will be finalized within the hour."

"Finalized unless I hand over my son to you," Jericho finished for him.

It wasn't Herschel who answered but rather Theo. "You don't have the right to raise that little boy."

Jericho was about to assure Theo and these other three that he did indeed have that right, but then he heard a sound he definitely didn't want to hear. The front door of the house opening.

And Laurel stepped onto the porch. She didn't stay on the porch, however. She marched down the steps toward them.

"Which part of *stay inside* didn't you hear me say?" Jericho whispered to her through clenched teeth.

"I can't let you fight my battles for me."

He would have liked to remind her this battle

wasn't just hers. It was for custody of Maddox. But there was no sense letting her father know they were still at odds.

"You'll be arrested soon," her father said. "I plan to wait here until the cops from Dallas show up and take you away in handcuffs."

So, the Dallas PD had drawn the short straw. They probably didn't know this was part of Herschel's sick plan—especially since there was almost certainly some evidence against Laurel. *Some.* Her father would have seen to that.

Too bad Herschel hadn't sought out help from the SAPD. Jericho's brother Levi could have possibly helped put an end to this already. Of course, Herschel was probably insisting the crime had taken place in the Dallas PD's jurisdiction.

"I guess this means I won't be going to a mental hospital," Laurel remarked. She folded her arms over her chest, faced their enemies head-on. Well, at least she wasn't looking afraid now. Just riled to the core.

"That was only if the warrant fell through," her father answered. "It didn't. But I can always use it as a backup."

"Or you can come to your senses and do the right thing," Theo said to Laurel.

When Theo took a step toward Laurel, Jericho drew his gun. Aimed it at the man. "First warning. Don't come closer. You don't get a second warning."

Theo's expression turned to iron, and his eyes were still narrowed when he looked at Laurel. "You can marry me and put an end to all of this."

"Marry you?" she repeated. "And that'll make the criminal charges and the insanity allegations go away? That's not going to happen."

"Then prepare yourself to go to jail," the lawyer said, her tone sassy enough to put Jericho's teeth on edge.

"I'm already tired of you and I barely know you. Get back in the limo," Jericho ordered her. "Teddy, shoot her if she manages to get her hands on a gun while she's in there."

Clearly, Nan wasn't accustomed to being put in her place. She cursed at him. A vanilla kind of profanity that a third grader would have used. But she got her butt back in the limo.

One down, three to go.

Jericho pointed to several heavily treed areas around the ranch and then got the attention of the other two ranch hands. "Keep watch, because our visitor here likes to hire killers. Which is why you should be inside," he added to Laurel.

"I'm staying put until they leave," Laurel insisted.

Of course she was. And besides tossing her over his shoulder and hauling her back into the house—something that Jericho briefly considered—there was no way to get her to budge. That meant he really needed to hurry this conversation along.

"All right, let's just get this out on the table," Jericho said to Theo. "Laurel's not marrying you." After clearing that up, he turned to Herschel. "And she's darn sure not going anywhere with you."

"Then be prepared for me to take custody of my grandson, because the warrant will include a court order for me to do just that."

Doubtful. Still, Herschel could have manipulated that some way, too. It didn't matter. Jericho usually didn't have a shades-of-gray approach to the law, but in his son's case, he'd make some exceptions.

"I'm Maddox's father," Jericho said, just in case these two nut jobs had forgotten that significant detail.

Hell. Herschel's smug look returned. "You have no legal right to him. Your name's not even on the birth certificate. Plus, I have DNA results that my own daughter gave me. Results that prove that Theo is the baby's father."

"Those results are a lie!" Laurel snapped.

"Are they?" Herschel's smug look got worse.

"You know they are. I couldn't put your name

on the birth certificate," Laurel whispered to Jericho. "I couldn't let my father know. And I would have had to let you know, too."

Yes, because she couldn't have added Jericho's name without his knowledge. Considering she thought it would be a death sentence for him, there was no way Laurel would have done that. But that blank space and the fake DNA results were going to give Theo some leverage.

If Jericho allowed it to happen.

He wouldn't.

Herschel shrugged. "It'll take a while for you to redo the DNA test. Until then, Theo has a right to take his son. Go inside, Theo, and get Maddox. You know he's in that house."

"And I have a right to shoot Theo if he tries to go inside," Jericho insisted right back.

Maybe Theo wasn't so stupid, after all, because he didn't make a move. "We'll be back when that court order arrives, and Herschel and I will take custody."

Jericho wanted to use the cliché *over my dead body*, but since that's exactly what someone wanted, he kept it to himself. Besides, he didn't need to say anything. Herschel knew what kind of man Jericho was, and even with all this bluster and talk, he also knew Jericho wouldn't just hand the child over to Theo or him.

"Think of the danger," Theo said, looking at Laurel now. "Someone's obviously trying to kill Jericho and you. Maddox shouldn't be near you, or he could get caught in the crossfire."

"He's already been caught in it." And that's all Laurel said for several moments. The anger was there in her voice, but there was also plenty of hatred. "If you're so concerned about his safety, then come clean and tell us who's behind the attacks."

She stared at her father, maybe waiting for Theo to acknowledge in some way that Herschel was responsible.

Theo didn't utter a word.

But Herschel did. "I'm not trying to kill you."

"Then who is?" Laurel pressed.

Herschel blew out a long breath, rubbed the space between his eyebrows as if fending off a headache. "Maybe someone involved in that money laundering deal you orchestrated."

"I didn't orchestrate it. I was set up, probably by you. So, who other than you would want me dead?"

"Dorothy," Herschel finally admitted.

Theo opened his mouth as if to deny that, but he only shook his head. "Maybe," he conceded.

What Theo didn't concede, however, was that

he had just as much, if not more, motive than his mother. Something he'd never admit.

This was another of those not-over-my-dead-body situations. One they'd never resolve. But in the meantime, the minutes were just ticking away, and if Herschel was telling the truth, it wouldn't be long before the Dallas police arrived. That meant Jericho had to get Laurel and Maddox out of there fast.

"Come on." Jericho slipped his arm around Laurel's waist and got her moving toward the house.

"You can't run!" Herschel called out to them. "I have someone watching the ranch and the roads. Of course, if you try to run, I can have you charged with obstruction of justice. Then, Theo won't have any trouble claiming that boy."

Jericho didn't trade barbs with the man. Didn't even acknowledge him. He just hurried Laurel inside.

"Get Maddox's things," Jericho told her once he'd shut the door.

Her eyes widened for a moment. "We're leaving?"

"Yeah. Herschel might be watching the roads, but we can get out to the highway using the old ranch trails." Jericho didn't see another way around leaving.

Another way around something else that had to be done, too.

"We're going to a safe house," Jericho told her. "And then we're getting married—*today*."

Chapter Eight

As a young girl, Laurel had fantasized about her wedding.

To Jericho, of course.

However, she hadn't imagined her wedding would happen while she was wearing jeans, a purple top and while hiding out in a safe house. In her fantasy, Jericho hadn't been scowling, either.

Too bad that was what he'd been doing a lot since they'd arrived at the safe house. Of course, there was plenty to scowl about.

Moving her from the ranch and hiding her wouldn't put him in the good graces of the Dallas PD. Something that clearly didn't please him since he'd been the sheriff of Appaloosa Pass for well over a decade. This had also put his brothers in a bind since they, too, were lawmen, and the Dallas PD would be pressing each one of them to tell them where Jericho had taken her.

They wouldn't tell.

His brothers were loyal to him.

But that didn't mean this kind of pressure couldn't hurt their careers. Plus, as long as there was danger of an attack, Jericho's family would have to continue watching their backs. Because the person after them could use Jericho's family to get to him.

She definitely wasn't getting on their good sides like this.

The only upside to this was that for the moment Maddox was safe. And this marriage would ensure his safety even if she was arrested.

Laurel checked her hair in the dresser mirror. Yes, it was silly to be concerned with such things, but it was her wedding day, after all. Her hair was fine, but there was no way she could conceal the worry in her eyes.

Thank goodness Maddox was too young to notice it, and so far he'd acted as if coming to the safe house was an adventure. Laurel could partly thank Iris for that. Jericho's mother had come with them. Along with Levi. Iris and Levi had spent the past couple of hours entertaining him in the large family room of the rural ranch house.

Jericho, too.

She wasn't sure why she was surprised by it, but Jericho seemed to slide right into daddy mode. And it wasn't as if he didn't have other things to do. He had plenty, what with all the arrangements for the so-called wedding, and for transferring custody of Maddox to him. Jericho had taken care of those things. Had continued to get updates about the investigation and some other cases he was in the middle of.

But it certainly felt as if he'd put Maddox first.

Since her bedroom door wasn't shut, Laurel had no trouble hearing the footsteps in the hall, and a moment later Jericho appeared in the doorway.

Still scowling.

Like her, he was dressed casually, wearing jeans and a gray button-up shirt.

"How's Maddox?" she asked.

"Napping on a quilt in the family room."

Not unusual since Maddox still took two naps a day. At least they'd managed to maintain parts of his routine.

"I think we tired him out," Jericho added. "Does he always have that much energy?"

"Always. Between him and me, you won't be getting much sleep for a while." She winced because that sounded a little more intimate than she'd intended.

Thankfully, Jericho ignored it and glanced in the direction of the family room. No doubt where his mother and Levi still were, before he stepped inside and shut the door.

"The justice of the peace will be here in about

an hour," he explained. "Keep your fingers crossed that the weather cooperates."

Yes, that. As if they needed more obstacles. The sky was iron-gray, and it was cold. Anything that fell now was more likely to be ice than snow. A white Christmas was rare in this part of the state. However, ice could definitely slow down or even stop the justice of the peace from getting out to the safe house.

"You trust this person?" she asked.

Jericho nodded. "Jax will be driving him out and will make sure they aren't followed."

Good. Jericho had already told her that only a handful of people, mostly his family and his deputies, knew about the location of the safe house. It wasn't one that any other law enforcement agencies used but rather belonged to a friend of one of the deputies.

"I've also started the paperwork for you to sign over custody of Maddox to me," Jericho added.

That was what Laurel wanted. Or rather what she needed to happen. Still, it felt like a punch, and the doubts came. So did the tears that she tried to blink back.

"Your family hates me," she said.

"Yeah, they do. But that has nothing to do with giving me custody. I'm doing this to stop Herschel, not to claim Maddox."

Laurel heard the accusation in his voice, and it

was there for a good reason. She'd kept Maddox from him. "What I did was wrong. But please believe me, I thought I was doing the right thing."

Jericho didn't give her any indication he agreed with that. The pain was still too raw over having been shut out of his son's life for eighteen months. Maybe it always would be. The current situation certainly wasn't helping matters.

He glanced at her. Specifically at her tear-filled eyes. He mumbled something she didn't catch, and as if it was the last thing on earth he wanted to do, Jericho slipped his arm around her. Pulled her to him.

Laurel hated that it was a dose of instant comfort.

Instant attraction, too.

He made a sound deep within his chest, and backed away. Physically, he did, anyway. The attraction was still there. His scowl, too, though he had toned it down at bit. It made her wonder, though, if it'd ever go away.

"You don't really want to do this with me," she said.

"What?" No scowl, just some confusion in his eyes. "The marriage? Or…"

"Of course. Oh." They were talking about the forbidden attraction now. The kind of attraction that would cause a rift the size of Texas in his family. "Nothing will happen. We've got this under control."

Laurel hadn't realized Jericho would take that as a challenge, and maybe he hadn't wanted it to be one. He cursed again. Not general cursing, either. It had her name in it. And judging from the profanity, she thought he was about to call off the wedding and storm out of there.

He didn't.

Still cursing her, and adding some raw words for himself, Jericho took hold of both her arms and snapped her to him. Laurel didn't even manage a sound of protest before his mouth was on hers.

The feelings came in a flash. The memories and the attraction. Always the attraction. But the pleasure was there, too, simmering right along with other things—including the reminder that this wasn't a good thing for them to be doing.

Her body didn't listen.

It never listened when it came to Jericho.

For just a couple of moments, she wanted to get lost in the pleasure. In the kiss. Not hard to do. The heat warmed her from head to toe. His mouth took the heat to a slow burn, and it didn't take long for Laurel to do something about that. She slipped her arms around his neck and pulled him closer.

He had the beginnings of an erection. She

found that out when she brushed against him. That should have been a big red flag to put a stop to this, but her body seemed to think it was a good thing. Jericho still wanted her. Of course, the deep kiss was already proof of that. She got more proof when he dropped some of those kisses on her neck.

And lower.

Mercy, she wanted him to go lower.

More profanity from him. Not exactly traditional foreplay, but then this wasn't foreplay.

Was it?

She tested that by brushing her sex against his.

All right, it felt like foreplay, which meant it had to end. There was no way she could have sex—

Jericho groaned and jammed his hand between them to block the *foreplay*. Not a good idea because it meant his hand was practically between her legs. Exactly where that part of her wanted it to be.

Without warning, Jericho turned her, pressing the front of her against the door. And pressing his body against her back. Definitely not the way to continue the foreplay.

Or so she thought.

It slowed things down. No more frantic kisses. No more testing the limits of his jeans by brushing against his erection.

But the kissing didn't stop.

With his breath gusting and hot on her skin, Jericho cupped her chin with his left hand and kissed the back of her neck. He kept his other hand on her lower stomach, and he lowered it even more. Touching her until Laurel's vision blurred and she lost what little breath she had.

She didn't get a chance to regain her breath because Jericho pressed himself, hard and hot, against her. And just when Laurel was within a heartbeat of an orgasm, he stepped back.

All the way back.

So that no part of him was touching any part of her.

Laurel stayed there a moment. Not wanting to face him. But knowing she couldn't put that off forever. She eased around, fixing her clothes to avoid eye contact with him. However, Jericho forced that, too, by catching onto her chin again.

"Yeah, we've got it all under control," he snapped. "I don't think it's a good sign when we start lying to ourselves."

No. But then making out with him wasn't a good sign, either.

She glanced at his zipper area. "Are you going to do something about that?" Good grief. "I mean, you can't go out there like that."

"And you can't go out there like that." He

dropped his gaze to her breasts. Her nipples were still hard and pressed against her top.

Since there wasn't much else she could do, Laurel laughed. Not actually from humor. More from the absurdity of this. "Guess we're both wearing our lust on our sleeves."

"We always have." He scrubbed his hand over his face. "Look, we can go ahead and finish what we started, but it'd be a mistake. Agreed?"

"Yes."

She couldn't say it fast enough. Especially not with his brother and mother just a few walls away. Mothers and siblings tended to have a sixth sense about that sort of thing, and she already had enough on her plate without incurring another dose of Crockett anger.

Since some of that anger would also be aimed at Jericho.

They would forgive him, eventually, for fathering a child with her, but that forgiveness wouldn't extend to starting up their relationship again.

"I should check on Maddox," she said, though she knew he was fine. Laurel just didn't want Iris and Levi to notice that Jericho and she had been behind a closed door for much too long.

"Do we look guilty of…something?" Laurel asked him as she opened the door.

He didn't answer, other than emit a soft grunt, which let her know they did indeed look guilty.

They went into the family room, and yes, both Levi and Iris were still there. Levi was at the window, keeping watch, but he glanced in her direction, giving her one of those Crockett snarls. He was like Jericho in so many ways. Just slightly less intense. But he made sure she got some of that intensity.

Iris, too.

Except her expression was one of apprehension. She stood, facing Jericho. "Are you sure this marriage is the only way?" Iris asked.

"It's the fastest way," Jericho assured her. "If all goes well, I'll have custody of Maddox in a day or two, and then we can focus fully on dealing with Laurel's legal issues. We're already working on that, but Herschel has a lot of judges and important people in his pocket."

"Maybe a lot of hired guns, too," Laurel added.

"Maybe?" Iris questioned. Despite the truce Iris had offered, it was clear it was going to take a while for the woman to fully trust Laurel. "Even now you doubt him."

Laurel looked her straight in the eye. "No. I don't. I know what he is, but there are other suspects. Theo and his mother. Plus, it might be someone who's upset about the business deals that fell through when I broke off my engagement with Theo."

Obviously, Iris wasn't buying any of that. And she might be right. Her father was certainly the top suspect for the attacks, and that's the main reason Laurel didn't want to exclude the others. Someone, like Theo, could be using this to get revenge on her while her father would get the blame.

"I don't like this." Iris shook her head, looked at Jericho. "If you're her husband and if it comes up that she knows something about Herschel murdering your father, then you can't testify against her."

Oh, so that was the reason Iris was worrying. Well, one reason, anyway. The bad blood was playing into this, too.

"As my husband, Jericho can't be forced to testify. But if Jericho found anything, I'm sure he would testify even if it meant putting me behind bars." That kiss had made her weak in the knees, but she wasn't delusional. "I promise you, though, I had nothing to do with your husband's murder."

Iris's chin came up. "But you never tried to have your father convicted of it, either."

"True. I looked, but I didn't look hard enough." Because she'd known that her father would get back at her through her mother.

And he had.

"Mom," Levi said, "it's okay. Jericho knows what he's doing." However, despite the lack of bite in his voice, Levi didn't sound any more convinced than Iris looked.

Jericho's phone buzzed, and she saw Dexter's name on the screen. Laurel hoped the deputy wasn't calling with another round of bad news. Jericho went into the kitchen to take the call, and Laurel followed him. This time, he put the call on speaker. Probably because he didn't want any more close contact with her. After what had just happened in the bedroom, that wasn't a bad idea.

"Jericho, we've got a problem," Dexter greeted. "There were just two cops here from the Dallas PD, and they were looking for Laurel and you. I told them I didn't know where you were."

"Thanks." Jericho paused. "What else did they say?" he asked, because he no doubt heard the hesitation in his deputy's voice.

"I tried to buy you some time. Said I'd need a day or two to find you. But they didn't believe that. They left, but they said they'd be back. They're giving you six hours to turn over Laurel, or they'll swear out a warrant for your arrest. And for me and all the other deputies. They said they'd get the Texas Rangers in here to take over the whole sheriff's office."

Jericho said a single word of profanity under

his breath. Laurel silently said a whole lot more. She didn't want anyone to go to jail to protect her, but she also didn't want to hand over her son to her father.

"I'll handle this," Jericho assured Dexter at the same time that Levi called out from the living room. "Jax and the justice of the peace are here."

"Good." Though there was nothing in Jericho's body language that indicated anything about this latest news was *good.* "I'll phone you back," he added to Dexter, and he ended the call.

"I'll have to turn myself in," Laurel insisted. And her mind began to whirl with the possibilities of how to do that while keeping Maddox safe.

Jericho gave her a look that could have withered an entire forest, and he took hold of her hand to lead her back into the living room. "Come on. Once the vows are finished, we'll work out what the hell we're going to do."

Chapter Nine

Jericho checked the time. Laurel and he had been married exactly one hour, and he was already on his sixth phone call. He'd never really given much thought to his wedding day, but he sure as heck hadn't figured that he'd be spending his time trying to keep himself and his entire department out of jail.

But that's exactly what he was doing.

Along with putting some things into motion that he hoped would buy Laurel and him some time. Time he needed, because the only way to put a stop to this situation was to find the link between those hired thugs and Herschel.

"I might have something," Levi said the moment Jericho finished his latest call.

Since Levi, too, was working on his own string of phone conversations, Jericho hoped his brother had a whole lot better news than he did.

"It's about Rossman and Cawley," Levi explained. "The FBI wiretapped their office months ago and recorded all their calls. There are several from Laurel to discuss a real estate transaction. But there's one from a man who doesn't identify himself. It could be Herschel. There's nothing that out and out incriminates him. Only one sentence—'Let's get this done.' If it's Herschel's voice, then we'll at least have proof that he was in on the deal."

"You can access my phone messages if you need a sample of my father's voice to compare to the recording," Laurel said, walking into the kitchen. She'd obviously been listening. "I don't have my phone with me. Jericho said maybe it could be traced, so I took out the memory card and left it at the ranch."

"I can access your phone messages from here," Levi assured her.

She blew out a breath of relief and turned her attention to Jericho. Laurel was obviously waiting for good news. Too bad Jericho didn't have a string of good news to give Levi or her. But he did have something.

"The custody papers have been filed," Jericho explained to them. "They're being walked through, so they'll be done before the judge and his staff leave for Christmas break."

Jericho hoped. That was the plan, anyway, but it was possible that key players needed for the process had already left work for the holidays.

"Good," Laurel said under her breath and then repeated it. "And what about the arrest warrants for you and the deputies?"

Jericho looked at Levi, hoping he'd made some progress in that area. But Levi shook his head. "The warrants haven't been sworn out yet, but the Dallas PD has probable cause if they believe you're harboring a fugitive."

Yep, there it was in a nutshell. He was indeed doing just that. And in this case, he was now married to the fugitive.

His *wife*.

The word didn't exactly stick in Jericho's throat, but it was close. He'd had no plans for marriage, but he'd always thought when and if he got around to saying I do, that it wouldn't have been to save his son. Or to save Laurel.

"I'm really sorry," she said as if she knew exactly what he was thinking.

"Don't," Jericho warned her. He would have liked to have added that this wasn't of her own making. But that was only partly true. She had brought some of this mess on herself by not seeing the truth about her father sooner.

She didn't listen to his warning. "I'm sorry," she repeated. First to Jericho. Then to Levi. "How much time do we have before I turn myself in and stop those arrest warrants from being issued?"

"I've already told you, that's not going to happen," Jericho snapped.

"No, you glared at me when I said I was going to do it. Now that you've got the custody papers started, I can turn myself in."

Jericho got to his feet so he could make eye contact with her and so she could see that he wasn't leaving room for argument. "Your father's past the brow-beating stage with you. He wants you behind bars, and he wants Maddox. Turning yourself in won't stop that."

Laurel lifted her hands in the air. "Then how do we stop him?"

He had a plan, all right. Jericho just wished it was a whole lot better than it was. "I've asked the county sheriff to file charges against Herschel for trespassing on the ranch."

Levi looked at him as if he'd sprouted an extra nose. "That won't put Herschel behind bars."

"No, but it'll keep him occupied for a few hours while he's trying to sort it out." Maybe. "In the meantime, Jax and Weston are digging into the backgrounds on the shrinks who gave fake reports regarding your mental health. They're looking to find a way to connect Herschel to the illegal activity."

Laurel didn't exactly jump for joy. Probably because she knew her father would have covered his tracks well.

"Chase will help them when he can, but he's on a lead right now to find the Moonlight Strangler," Jericho added.

He hated he couldn't pull Chase away from that case, but it was critical that the Moonlight Strangler be stopped. Especially since the snake would no doubt strike again. And soon.

She stayed quiet for a few seconds before her gaze drifted toward the living room. "Maddox deserves better than this," she whispered.

Yeah. He did. A whole lot better.

Jericho didn't know a lot about babies, but he knew this should be a time of celebration. Presents, Christmas trees, lots of excitement. Well, there was excitement, all right, but it was the wrong kind.

"I'll make sure he has some gifts," Jericho assured her. He wasn't certain how he would manage that, yet, but he'd get him something even if he had to download some games and books from the internet.

Levi must have decided this wasn't a conversation he needed to be in on, because he took out his phone again and headed out of the kitchen. "I'll see what I can do about speeding up the process for that voice comparison."

Jericho thanked his brother, was ready to launch into some calls himself, but he stood so he could glance into the living room and check on Maddox. Still asleep. So was his mother. She was napping in the recliner next to Maddox.

He went closer, his attention on his son's face, and he wondered if it would always be like this when he looked at him. That strong wash of love. So strong that it seemed to crush his chest. Twenty-four hours ago, Jericho hadn't even known Maddox existed, and now he couldn't imagine a life without him.

That meant a life with Laurel, too.

Even after they put an end to the danger and sorted out all her legal troubles, she would still be in his life. Jericho was guessing she'd want some kind of split-custody arrangement. And maybe that'd work. But he didn't want to lose another minute with his son, much less the time he wouldn't have with Maddox if he had to share custody with Laurel.

He glanced at Laurel and realized she was staring at him. "What?" Jericho asked.

"Magical, huh? I mean, people tell you what it's like to love a child, but you can't imagine it until it happens to you."

Jericho didn't trust his voice and settled for a nod. But Laurel kept staring. "Something else on your mind?"

She waved it off, literally, but then shook her head. "You didn't cough or choke when you said I do."

"Neither did you."

"It was different for me." Laurel sank down in the chair across from him. "You're the one doing me the favor. I wanted the marriage."

"This isn't a favor." Or a real marriage, for that matter. "I did this for my son." Which seemed a stupid thing to say since Laurel was doing it for the same reason.

She nodded. Paused, then nodded again. "Did you keep your blue rock?"

Now, here was the part where he could be ornery and say no, that he didn't have a clue what'd happened to it. But considering that he and Laurel had been through hell and back, it didn't seem fair.

"Yeah. It's in the junk drawer in the kitchen."

"A good place for it." And yes, there was a touch of sarcasm in her tone.

"I was going to toss it, changed my mind, and the drawer was nearby."

Best not to tell her that he also kept his father's badge in that drawer. And some family photos. A drawer he walked by and saw every time he came in and out of his house.

"It was a silly memento, anyway," Laurel added.

She looked up at him, their gazes connecting, and it seemed as if a dozen things passed between them without them saying a word. Of course, most of those dozen things included the puppy-love kisses when they'd found those rocks.

And the lust-induced kissing session they'd had just before the wedding.

Nothing puppy love about that.

Hell, he still was having trouble walking. He didn't want to know how long it'd be for the memory of her taste to fade.

Maybe never.

Since this wasn't something he wanted on his mind, Jericho was thankful when his phone buzzed. That thankfulness didn't last long, though, when he saw Theo's name on the screen.

"I'll take this in the bedroom so I don't wake up Maddox and Mom," Jericho said, showing Laurel the screen.

She followed him, of course, and once Jericho was in his bedroom with the door shut, he put the call on speaker.

"Where are you?" Theo demanded the moment Jericho answered.

"Really? You think that's any of your business?"

"It's my business because I'm worried about Laurel. Is she with you?"

"Again, none of your business. And if this is the only reason you called, then you're wasting my time and yours—"

"It's not the only reason." But Theo didn't

exactly hurry to continue that explanation. "I found something. About Herschel."

Laurel opened her mouth, no doubt to ask what, but Jericho shook his head. Even though Theo no doubt thought they were together, Jericho didn't want to confirm that for him.

"What'd you find?" Jericho snapped. "And this better not be a waste of my time."

"It's not a waste." Still, Theo took several moments to add something to that. "Herschel had fake psychiatric evaluations done on Laurel."

This time, Jericho huffed. "Tell me something I don't know. Laurel's sane. Herschel's not. Of course he faked them."

"Yes, but I can prove it."

Laurel's gaze flew to his, and he saw the hope in her eyes. Hope that Jericho wasn't ready to feel just yet. After all, this was Theo. And it wasn't jealousy playing into his dislike of the man. Well, maybe it was still a small part of it, but Jericho didn't trust anyone who was in cahoots with Herschel.

"How can you prove it?" Jericho pressed.

"I talked to the psychiatrist, and then sent a follow-up email. He admitted in a roundabout way that he never even saw Laurel for evaluation."

That hope in Laurel's eyes got even stronger, but thankfully she stayed quiet.

"The shrink put that in writing?" Jericho asked.

"Yes, in an email. But it's not an outright admission of wrongdoing. He just says he made his recommendation based on the medical records Herschel provided to him."

Fake records, no doubt. "I want that email," Jericho ordered.

"I figured you would. It might not keep Laurel out of jail, but you could perhaps use it to discredit Herschel in some way."

Oh, yeah. And he could do that by giving it to the press.

"But the email's not all I have," Theo added. "Herschel's using two reports by two different psychiatrists, and I believe I can discredit the other one, as well."

Jericho didn't care for the way Theo let that hang in the air for a while. "I'm guessing you want something in exchange for this?" Jericho asked.

"I want to talk to Laurel. Face-to-face."

Hell. Jericho figured there'd be a catch. "You're withholding evidence in an active criminal investigation. I can have you charged with obstruction of justice if you don't turn over the information."

"You could, but I could also destroy the evidence, and Laurel could end up in a mental hospital or jail for years. I doubt either you or Laurel want that."

He didn't, but Jericho didn't want to deal with this snake, either. "Why is it so important for you to speak to Laurel?"

"There are things I need to tell her, and I can't do it over the phone."

Probably a ploy to try to win her back so he could salvage those business deals. Or maybe Theo did love her in his own sick way.

"As you can imagine, it's not a good idea for Laurel to be meeting anyone right now," Jericho reminded him. "Including you."

"I know about the arrest warrant for you and your deputies. I know you have a matter of only a few hours to turn her in or you'll be taken into custody, too. It's my guess neither Laurel nor you want that to happen." Theo didn't wait for confirmation. "So, meet me at the sheriff's office in Appaloosa Pass this afternoon. I can talk to Laurel before the deadline for you to turn her over to the Dallas PD."

Jericho stared at her. That hope was still there in her eyes, but this was hope with a big string attached. He didn't want her to have to deal with Theo. Hell, he didn't want her arrested.

"Why should I believe that you're willing to throw Herschel to the wolves?" Jericho asked.

Another long pause from Theo. "Because I don't think this is the way to change Laurel's mind."

"It's not. But you've gone along with it so far."

"Let's just say I've had a change of heart. The plan was never for Laurel to be put in danger."

"Really? Then, what was the plan?"

"I'll tell Laurel when I see her. And I'm emphasizing that *her* because if she's not there, then I won't be, either. The only way you're going to get what I have is for us to meet face-to-face."

"All right," Laurel said, moving closer to the phone. "I'll do it. I'll meet you at the sheriff's office in a couple of hours, you and I can talk, and then you can give us the evidence."

Jericho didn't bother to curse because he'd known this was what she'd do. He didn't like it, but then there wasn't much he liked about this, especially since he was still trying to prevent that arrest by completely clearing Laurel's name.

"Good. I'll see you both then." And Theo ended the call before Jericho could say anything else.

"I have to do this," Laurel immediately argued. "I've known all along I'd have to turn myself in before the deadline the Dallas PD gave us. I can't risk having you arrested, not when we're so close to you getting custody of Maddox."

Part of that made some sense, though it was a bitter pill to swallow. He didn't want to think of Laurel in jail even for a short period of time.

"I don't want Maddox near Theo," Jericho insisted.

"Neither do I. Maybe he can stay here with your mother, Levi and one of the deputies."

Jericho would make sure there was at least one deputy at this safe house, and he would do whatever else it took to protect Maddox.

"When I'm arrested, I'll need you to bail me out," she added.

He would, of course, but she'd still have those mental-instability accusations hanging over her head. The mental instability could cancel out the other charges, since a lawyer could argue that if she was indeed crazy, then she wasn't fit to stand trial for money laundering. Either way, though, Laurel would be locked up somewhere until Jericho could prove she should be set free.

"What does Theo want to talk to you about?" he came out and asked.

She blew out a long breath, pushed her hair from her face. "He probably just wants to try to win me back. He can't."

"Obviously. You're married to me now, so that shoots to hell his notion of winning you back." He paused. "Doesn't it?"

That got him a huff and an eye roll. "Now

that I know we can keep Maddox from my father, nothing would make me go back to Theo. *Nothing.*"

There weren't any doubts in her voice. And that got Jericho thinking about something else she'd let slip the day before.

"You said Theo wasn't your lover. Explain that."

"Your memory is a little too good." She sighed, looked away, dodging his gaze. "Theo knew I didn't love him, but I agreed to the engagement to get my father off my back. And my mother's. My father was always pressuring her to pressure me, and I finally just gave in and said yes. I know, that makes me weak."

He didn't verbally argue with that, but he made to let her know he didn't totally agree. "And the part about him not being your lover?"

Laurel shrugged. "I told Theo we'd have to wait until we were married before we had sex."

"And he agreed to that?"

"I didn't give him a choice."

Well, great day. "He didn't press you to change your mind?"

"He did. I stopped him." She glanced away again, but when her attention came back to him, there was a little fire in her eyes. "Satisfied?"

Jericho played around with some answers to

that and decided there wasn't a good one. Was he satisfied she hadn't slept with Theo?

Yeah.

And yeah, that made him somewhat of a jerk.

"Theo might have had the hots for you, but I still believe it's mostly about business when it comes to you," Jericho settled for saying. "So yes, I guess I am satisfied that you didn't end up in bed with a man who wanted to use you."

No more gaze dodging. She stared at him. "And that's the only reason you're *satisfied*?"

No. Laurel knew that, too, because of those scalding kisses they'd just shared. Kisses he could still feel in every inch of him.

He was betting she could feel them, too, because her breathing became uneven, and her face flushed.

"Don't answer that," she insisted. "It's technically our wedding night, and please don't say or do anything that would make me want to get in your bed."

Jericho was about to make a big mistake and point out that'd there be a lot of wanting going on tonight, whether she was in his bed or not. Of course, admitting that want would be the very thing that would make them forget all of the damage they could do by sleeping together again. Thankfully, he was saved from saying something like that because of the knock at the door.

"Jericho," Levi said, "we have a problem."

Heck. What now? Jericho hurried to the door and threw it open. Even if his brother hadn't mentioned something was wrong, he would have been able to tell just by looking at Levi's face.

"Jax and the other deputies are on their way back out here and will be here any minute. We'll need to leave as soon as they get here." There was just as much concern in Levi's voice as there was in his expression. "Jax believes our location has been compromised."

Chapter Ten

Laurel's heart went to her knees. No. This couldn't be happening. Her baby was in danger again.

"Grab your things and Maddox's diaper bag," Jericho told her. He didn't seem nearly as shaky as she was, but Laurel figured he was just as concerned.

"How did this happen?" she asked, hurrying across the hall to her room. Thankfully, the house wasn't so large that she couldn't hear Levi's answer.

"When Jax picked up the justice of the peace, he told him to leave his phone behind, that it could be traced. Well, he left his business one but forgot he had his personal one in his briefcase."

All right, that wasn't as bad as the wild ideas running through her head. Ideas of kidnappers and gunmen on the way. Still, Jax was right and most cell phones could be tracked.

"Jax is pretty sure that someone, maybe

Herschel, hired people to watch all the justices of the peace in the area. Ministers, too. Jax knows they weren't followed, but if the spy saw the JP leave with Jax, then they could have tapped into the GPS tracker on his phone."

So, moving was just a precaution. That didn't cause Laurel to slow down, though. It was best to get Maddox away from here.

"Jax and the deputies are here," Iris called out to them.

That sent Levi hurrying to the living room. With her own bag and the diaper bag in hand, Laurel was about to head there, too, but Jericho stopped her in the hall. Now she saw more emotion on his face, and she knew he was about to tell her something she didn't want to hear.

"I need to go to the office and meet with Theo," Jericho said. "You're still sure you want to come with me?"

"Of course. Theo won't give us the recording or anything else if I'm not there." And Laurel was positive that wasn't a bluff. If she wasn't there, they wouldn't get the proof that could clear her of the false psychiatric reports.

If Theo actually had a recording, that is.

Theo likely had something. Something that he was sure he could use to get her to talk to him. Laurel only hoped it was worth the risk and the emotional toll it would take for her to be away from Maddox. Even though she hoped she wouldn't have to be away from him for too long.

"How will this work?" she asked Jericho.

He scrubbed his hand over his face. Clearly frustrated. "I'll have Jax and the deputies take Mom and Maddox to a new location. Another safe house. Levi, you and I can go to the office."

"Levi could go with them, too," she suggested.

"No way. I want backup with us when we're on the road."

Laurel nodded, finally, and with that green light given, Jericho rushed her back into the living room. Iris already had Maddox bundled in her arms, ready to go. Her son was still half asleep, but he smiled when he looked at her. His smile got even bigger when he looked at Jericho.

"Tar," Maddox muttered, pointing to Jericho's badge.

Jericho returned the smile and stepped away to tell the others the plan. Laurel used the time to say goodbye to her son.

"Be a good boy for Mommy." She pressed some kisses on his cheek. "I'll see you soon." Laurel hoped. It was possible that it would be days, since, with the holidays, it might not be easy for Jericho to post bond for her.

"I'll take good care of him," Iris assured her.

"Thank you." And she meant it. It was easy to see that Iris loved Maddox. Jericho, too. That

would make it easier for him if things turned
from bad to worse and Laurel ended up with a
long jail sentence.

"You ready?" Jericho asked her when he'd finished talking to his brothers and the deputies.

Laurel nodded. Kissed Maddox again. Jericho did the same, brushing a kiss on his forehead. That was it, the only goodbye before he
got them outside.

Jax had parked an SUV directly in front of the
door, and Laurel was relieved when she saw the
infant seat. It probably belonged to his own son
since this was Jax's personal vehicle.

Iris got Maddox strapped in, with Dexter getting into the backseat with them. Jax and Mack
took the front seat, and Jax didn't waste any time
speeding away.

"Best to get moving," Levi reminded them,
and they hurried to his truck on the side of the
house.

It was still bitterly cold, but thankfully there
was no ice or snow falling. Not yet. Maybe it
wouldn't start until Maddox and the others had
arrived at the new place. She definitely didn't
want her baby on icy roads.

Laurel kept her gaze nailed to Jax's SUV,
watching it while she ran to the truck and got
on the seat between Levi and Jericho, with Levi
behind the wheel. She could have sworn a hand

squeezed around her heart when the SUV was out of sight.

"It'll be okay," Jericho said to her.

She hated that the tears came, but this had been an emotional overload of a day, and it wasn't over yet. "Please tell me the new place will be safe."

"It will be." Almost idly, Jericho brushed a kiss on her forehead, much as he'd done to Maddox just minutes earlier.

Levi made a soft grunt. Probably of disapproval, and he took something from his pocket. A plain gold wedding band.

"Jax brought it with him," Levi said, passing it to Laurel. "He thought it would be a good idea for you to wear it."

Because her head was in such a muddle, Laurel looked at Jericho for an explanation.

"It might get Theo to back off. From pressuring you about getting back together with him, anyway. It might also help if you have to appear before a judge. It makes the marriage seem, well, real, and not something we slapped together so Herschel can't get Maddox."

Of course, the marriage had indeed been slapped together, and while it might not sway a judge, it was a nice finishing touch. Laurel slipped the ring on and then had a horrible thought.

"The ring doesn't belong to Jax's late wife,

Paige, does it?" Laurel knew Jax and Paige had divorced shortly before she'd been murdered, but the ring would still have sentimental value for Jax and Paige's son.

Levi shook his head. "It belonged to our grandmother. Jax meant to bring it with him when he drove out with the JP, but he forgot."

"I can't wear this. It's…real. It's a family heirloom." She started to take it off, but Jericho stopped her by sliding his hand over hers.

"Keep it on." He didn't add more than that. Didn't move his hand from hers, either.

Laurel hated that something as simple as Jericho's touch would help her calm down, but it did. However, it didn't do the same for Levi. Jericho's brother didn't say a thing, but she saw a flash of disapproval in his eyes. First the kiss, now this. Levi was probably ready to give her an earful.

But he didn't.

In fact, he didn't say anything, and that's when she noticed he was volleying his attention between the rearview mirror and the road ahead. Jericho was doing the same thing, but he took it one step further.

Jericho drew his gun.

That caused the skin to crawl on the back of her neck.

"What's wrong?" Laurel tried to turn and look

behind them, but she didn't get the chance. Jericho pushed her down on the seat.

"Maybe nothing."

However, it didn't feel like *nothing*.

"That person in the black SUV behind us could be following us," Levi supplied. "Let's find out."

That was the only warning she got before Levi made a left turn. And she waited. Breath held. Her mind and heart racing.

She wasn't familiar with this part of the county. It was all rural, just ranch land and woods, and from her position on the seat, Laurel could tell the road was bumpy, coiling its way through the trees that were practically a canopy over them.

"Hell," Jericho said. And she knew then that whoever had been behind them had made that same turn.

"Can you see how many are in the vehicle?" Levi asked.

Jericho shook his head. "The windows are too dark. Take that next turn. That'll get us headed toward Miller Road."

Which would lead them back into town. Eventually. By her estimation, they were at least twenty minutes out. Maybe more, since they were on the back roads.

Laurel forced herself to remember that this

could still turn out to be nothing. After all, it could be someone who lived in the area.

Levi took the next turn as Jericho had told him. And the wait began again. Laurel wasn't sure how time managed to crawl and fly by at the same time, but it felt as if that's what was happening.

Jericho cursed again and pushed her farther down on the seat. That meant they had their answer.

They were being followed.

And worse.

"Watch out!" Jericho shouted to his brother.

Just as the bullet slammed into the roof of the truck.

JERICHO DIDN'T HAVE time to curse. Though that's something he'd be doing plenty of later. For now, he had to do something to make sure all three of them got out of there alive.

"Just focus on the road," Jericho told his brother. "I'll see what I can do about the idiot who just fired that shot."

A shot that Jericho had barely seen coming. He hadn't noticed the passenger's-side window of the SUV was down, but he'd darn sure seen the person's hand snake out with that blasted gun. A gun he'd quickly used to fire a shot at them before pulling his hand back inside.

Jericho doubted it'd stay that way.

No, this was an attack, and it was clear from the shot that the thugs inside didn't care if they killed them or not.

Now, the question was—who had ordered the thugs to attack?

Jericho would find out, but first things first. He lowered his own window. Leaned out just enough to take aim. And he sent a shot right into the windshield of the SUV. The bullet slammed into the glass, creating a small circle, but it didn't go through, which meant their attackers had come prepared. The glass was bulletproof.

Unlike their truck.

And the thug must have known that because the passenger's hand came out again and he fired another shot.

This one slammed into the side of Jericho's door but, thankfully, ricocheted off. Of course, a ricocheted bullet could still hit one of them.

"I'm turning," Levi warned them a split second before he took a left on another farm road. Jericho wasn't familiar with this particular one, but most of the roads led back toward Appaloosa Pass. He hoped this one did because he didn't want to have to dodge bullets any longer than necessary.

"Maddox," Laurel said on a rise of breath. There was plenty of panic in her voice.

Plenty of panic inside Jericho, too. He prayed attackers hadn't gone after Maddox, as well.

"Call Jax," Jericho said, and tossed her his phone.

He glanced at her to make sure she stayed down when she did that. She did. And Jericho tried to tamp down his fears for his son while he kept an eye on the shooter behind them.

The guy didn't reach out again, probably because the road was a series of curves, and it would be nearly impossible to take aim. That was something, at least, but the curves probably wouldn't go on for long.

"Someone's shooting at us," Laurel said the moment Jax answered her call. "Is Maddox all right?"

How could just a few seconds seem like an eternity? Jericho wasn't close enough to hear Jax's answer, so he could only wait. And pray.

"They're okay," Laurel relayed. "No one's following them."

He released the breath he'd been holding, but Jericho didn't have time to celebrate his son's safety. The hand came out of the window again, and the shooter pulled the trigger. This time, though, the shot slammed into the rear windshield and sent the safety glass spewing right at them.

Jericho tried to cover Laurel as best he could.

Which wasn't much coverage at all. Still, the protective coating around the glass had saved them from getting cut to shreds. However, with the giant gaping hole, the bitter cold came in, and it didn't take long for the temp inside the truck to plummet.

"Another turn," Levi announced.

He took the turn on what had to be two tires, at best, and Jericho's heart thudded against his chest when the truck went into a skid. Levi quickly got control, thank God, but Jericho knew there wouldn't be much time before another bullet came their way.

"Jax wants to know how far we are from town," Laurel asked. She looked up at him, meeting his gaze for just a moment, and Jericho saw the terror in her eyes.

"About ten miles," Levi answered.

Even at the speed they were going, which was too fast for these curvy country roads, that was still way too much time for these idiots to take this situation from bad to worse.

Laurel passed along that information to Jax. "Jax will have someone tap into the GPS to get our location," she relayed when she ended the call. "He'll get backup out to us as fast as he can."

Jericho had no doubt his brother would do just

that, but it was a long shot for backup to arrive in time.

Which meant he had to do something now.

Jericho got a confirmation of that when another bullet came through the vehicle and bashed into the front windshield. Like the glass in the back, it didn't shatter, but it broke like a giant spiderweb, making it next to impossible for Levi to see.

"Stop when you can," Jericho instructed. "We need to try to put an end to this."

Levi nodded, knowing they didn't have another option. He couldn't drive blind on these roads, and he certainly couldn't stick his head out the side window to see.

"They'll try to kill us if you stop," she said, her voice trembling.

"They're already trying to kill us." And were doing too good of a job at it since two more shots came their way, both of them hitting the side of the truck. These shots were definitely lower, which meant the guy was probably trying to shoot out a tire or two.

"Levi, the second you stop, get your gun ready. Aim for their tires," Jericho instructed. Because two could play at this game. "Laurel, so help me God, you'd better stay down."

"But I could help you return fire. I know how to handle a gun."

The glare Jericho tossed her let her know that wasn't going to happen. Still, he didn't want her unarmed just in case things got even worse than they already were, so he threw open the glove compartment, took out a backup weapon that he knew Levi kept there and tossed it to her.

"Stay down," Jericho warned her again.

She did, and he hoped she didn't get up, no matter what. Of course, he couldn't swear she'd be completely safe, but he did know that he and Levi were darn good shots, and it'd be much easier to shoot these clowns if they both weren't in moving vehicles.

"I'd like to keep one of them alive," Jericho said to Levi, and his brother nodded.

Not that they'd had good luck when it came to getting the other thugs to talk, but one of these might. And if not, then maybe Jericho could force him to talk.

This had to end.

He couldn't continue to allow Laurel and Maddox to be in danger, and that meant he might end up bending the law by forcing the guy to cough up some answers.

"How about stopping there?" Levi tipped his head to a small clearing in front of a cattle gate. There was a cluster of trees just to the left and an irrigation ditch on the right.

"Do it," Jericho answered.

The words had hardly left his mouth when Levi hit the brakes, hard, and he skidded into the narrow clearing. But he didn't just park. He maneuvered the truck around so that it was facing the SUV head-on.

Using the truck doors for cover, they both got out. Both took aim at the SUV's front tires. The SUV driver slammed on his brakes just as Levi and Jericho fired into them. Jericho was positive his bullet went into the tire, but it didn't go flat.

Hell.

Probably puncture resistant. Yeah, these guys had come prepared. But they probably hadn't expected the Crockett brothers to take a stand.

The SUV tires squealed, digging into the asphalt until it came to a stop about ten yards from them. No one got out, but the driver did lower his window. He stayed inside so that Jericho couldn't see him. He probably wouldn't have recognized him, anyway, since these were almost certainly hired killers.

"Well?" Jericho called out.

He didn't wait for a response. Not that he would have gotten one, anyway. Hired guns usually weren't big on talking.

Jericho fired a shot into the SUV's engine. Finally. He hit something that wasn't reinforced, because the bullet went through. However, it didn't immediately disable it because the engine continued to run.

So, Jericho continued to shoot at it.

Levi did the same. And soon they had a barrage of bullets slamming into the SUV hood.

Jericho had to stop to slap another magazine into his gun, and he was in the process of taking aim again when the driver threw the SUV into Reverse and hit the accelerator. He peeled out of there, fast.

Doing the one thing Jericho didn't want them to do.

They were getting away.

Chapter Eleven

Laurel couldn't stop shivering. Something she'd been doing on the entire drive to the sheriff's office. And despite the ample heat in the building, she was still shivering, the cold going all the way to the bone.

Thanks to those latest gunmen, she had a new set of memories to give her nightmares and make her tremble. A new set of worries, too.

Because the gunmen had gotten away.

That meant they could return for another attempt to kill Jericho and her. Of course, Jericho and his brothers were trying to stop that, but Laurel had to wonder what the heck she could do to put an end to this.

Maybe turning herself in to the police would work.

Maybe.

Or maybe that would just make her an easier target to kill.

Either way, it wasn't a theory Jericho wanted

to test, and he'd spent the last half hour since their arrival at his office making calls to the Dallas PD. Trying to stop the warrant for her arrest. Judging from the amount of his profanity and his scowl, it wasn't going well.

"Here, try this." Levi handed Laurel a cup of coffee.

Laurel took a sip of the coffee, nearly choked on it. It would need a lot of improvement just to classify as horrible, but it was hot, and with the hopes it would take away her chill, she drank some more.

"We should have heard from Jax by now," she said.

Levi made a sound of disagreement. "He's just being cautious. Jax is driving around to make sure they aren't being followed before he goes to the safe house with Maddox."

Yes, Jax had already told her exactly that in the three calls she'd made to him. Laurel didn't dare make another so soon since he'd warned her with the last one that he needed to concentrate on his driving. The temps were dropping, and he wanted to be careful.

Laurel wanted that, as well, but more than anything, she just wanted her son to be safe.

"Jax will take good care of him," Levi added. "And Jericho will find whatever he needs to find to put an end to this."

She desperately wanted to believe that. But it was easy to lose hope when they'd come so close to dying again.

"What about the kidnapper already in custody?" Laurel asked. "Is he still not talking?"

Levi shook his head. "We do know his name is Otto Palmer. We got that from his prints, so he obviously has a record. I think he would have talked, but he got spooked after DeWitt's death. He probably thinks the same thing will happen to him."

Yes, that would spook anyone, especially since they still weren't sure if DeWitt had taken his own life or if his so-called lawyer had murdered him.

Jericho stood when he finished his latest call, and that seemed to be Levi's cue to start moving away from her. "I'll see if I can find out what's happening with Rossman and Cawley."

Good idea, since the pair was yet something else they had to deal with, especially if they could help clear her name of the money laundering charges. "How about the wiretap recording you're trying to match to my father's voice?"

"Still working on it. I'll let you know the minute the FBI lab calls me back." Levi went to a desk in the corner and started another call.

"Did they find those men who shot at us?" she asked Jericho.

"Afraid not. But the county sheriff and his deputies are still out looking."

That was probably the last thing they wanted to do right before the holidays, but that area had come under the jurisdiction of the county sheriff. That meant Levi, Jericho and she would soon have to write statements of the incident so there could be an official investigation.

As if that would help.

She was betting those men were well out of the reach of the law. For the time being, anyway.

"I ran the plates on the black SUV," he continued. "They're not registered, of course, which means they're fake, but I also alerted car repair shops that someone might be bringing in a vehicle that matched the description."

He was covering all the bases as best he could. She hated to take a glass-half-empty outlook on this, but a person who had enough money to hire multiple hit men probably wouldn't care about having a vehicle repaired. Especially one that could be traced back to him or her.

"You're shaking," Jericho said.

He went closer to her, and barely touching her, he put his hand on the small of her back to get her moving toward his office. Maybe because he thought it'd be warmer there. Or maybe because he realized she was on the verge of tears.

Of course, there could be another reason for the privacy.

"Do you have more bad news?" Laurel came out and asked.

He took a moment, put his hands on his hips. "Not as bad as it could be. Dallas PD won't kill the warrant against you, but they're giving me some more time. I told them you'd been shaken up pretty bad in the latest attack."

That certainly wasn't a lie. "How much time?"

"Tomorrow morning."

Laurel groaned. Tomorrow was Christmas, and she hadn't wanted to spend it being arrested. "And what about the warrant for your arrest?"

Jericho flexed his shoulders. "They're not killing that, either. The captain at Dallas PD insists if I don't turn you in, they'll arrest me, the deputies and then bring in the Rangers to take over the sheriff's office. But they're giving me until tomorrow, too."

What a mess. Jericho loved his badge. Loved being sheriff. And now he had to choose between it and her. Laurel figured she would always be on the losing end when it came to his badge.

"I'll bet you wish you'd never met me," she whispered.

"Some days." He paused. Looked at her. Cursed. "Not today, though."

He turned, and as if part of a dance, he slipped his arm around her, drawing her to him.

And he kissed her.

There it was. The heat. Jericho could take her from shivering to hot in a matter of seconds. But this was more than just the fire from the attraction. The pull seemed to go even deeper, and it slid through her, head to toe.

As always, his mouth was clever, tasting and taking at once. And Laurel let him. She just tried to hang on, bracing herself for the onslaught of need. It came, all right. It always did and made her long for a real marriage.

He deepened the kiss. Tightened his grip. It robbed her of her breath and any clear thoughts she should be having. Well, she did have one clear thought—about his bed—but that vanished when she heard the bell jangling. The sound let them know that they had a visitor.

"Stay here." Jericho pulled her behind him and drew his gun.

"Laurel?" Theo called out. "Are you here?"

She certainly hadn't forgotten about Theo's planned visit, but with everything else going on, Laurel hadn't realized it was time for him to arrive.

Jericho stepped into the hall, and Laurel could tell from the way he stiffened that something wasn't right. One glimpse in the reception area, and she understood why he'd had that reaction. Theo wasn't alone.

Dorothy was with him.

Since Dorothy was a suspect, and Theo hadn't mentioned bringing her along, Jericho had reason for concern. That was probably why he didn't holster his gun.

"Why is she here?" Jericho tipped his head to Dorothy.

"Because I need to talk to Laurel, too," the woman insisted.

Theo huffed. "She followed me. Or rather, her driver did. He's parked just outside, waiting for her."

Laurel had no idea why Theo would be keeping things from his mother. Nor did she care. She only wanted this to be a short, productive visit. "Did you bring the evidence?" she asked.

Theo held up a manila envelope. "I did. But you'll get it only after we talk. That was the deal."

"So, talk," Jericho snapped, and he stayed between Theo and her.

Well, partially. Laurel's hand wasn't hidden, and Dorothy's attention snapped right to the wedding ring she was wearing.

"Did you marry him?" Dorothy howled. "Did you actually marry this cowboy cop?"

"I did." And Laurel braced herself for their reactions.

She didn't have to wait long. Dorothy started shaking her head, mumbling how stupid Laurel was, and as if she'd gone weak in the knees, the woman sank down into one of the chairs.

Theo, however, just stared at Laurel, and by degrees, she saw the changes in his expression. Surprise, at first. Quickly followed by some disappointment and then the anger. His jaw went tight. His eyes narrowed. Levi didn't miss the reaction, either, because he also drew his gun.

"Why the hell did you marry him?" Theo asked. He stormed toward her, but Jericho stepped in front of him, blocking his path.

"Why the hell do you care why she did it?" Jericho retorted. "Laurel broke off your engagement. That means she's free to marry me or anybody else, for that matter."

"No!" Theo shouted. "She definitely wasn't free to marry you." He went from anger to enraged, and Laurel thought about grabbing that envelope from him before he did something stupid.

Like try to destroy it.

But Jericho did the grabbing for her. He

snatched it from Theo, and motioned for Levi to take it. Levi came across the room to do just that.

"Get started on that right away," Jericho told his brother without taking his narrowed gaze off Theo.

Theo, however, looked past Jericho, his glare fixed on her. "Do you think I'm saving you from going to jail so you can be with the likes of him?"

Oh, that was not the right thing to say, and Laurel took hold of Jericho's arm in case he was about to punch Theo. Not that she would have minded that. Theo deserved a good punch or two for the remark, but she didn't want a fight in the sheriff's office. Especially since they had other more important battles.

"The likes of him?" Laurel repeated. Because she wanted to calm things down, she tried not to glare at Theo. "He's my son's father, along with being the sheriff here. Seems like a good match to me."

"Well, it's not! He didn't even know about Maddox until you went running to him. You should have let it stay that way."

"And lose custody of Maddox to my father?" she snapped. "I don't think so."

It appeared to take Theo a moment to rein in his temper enough just so he could speak. "I would have taken custody of him while I helped you work through the charges."

Jericho took a step toward him, narrowing the already narrow space between them. "That was never going to happen. Maddox is my son, not yours. And Laurel is my wife."

She could tell Theo wanted to start that fight with Jericho. One that he wouldn't win. Jericho didn't just look dangerous.

He *was* dangerous.

"Did you sleep with him, too?" Theo snarled.

Nearly. And part of Laurel wanted to throw that at Theo, but it would be like gasoline on a fire, and she was too exhausted to drag out this argument.

"What I do with Jericho is my business," she settled for saying. Still a bit of gasoline, but anything she could have said probably would have been. Theo was spoiling for a fight.

The trick would be to make sure Jericho didn't give him one.

"I loved you," Theo said to her. "I loved you more than anyone or anything ever. And I would have done whatever it took to protect you. You should have trusted me to deal with your father."

"How? By marrying me? Because that's what triggered all of this," Laurel reminded him. "I ended things between us and all hell broke loose. I have to believe you're at least partially responsible for that."

Theo didn't deny it. Not with words, anyway. But the look he gave her was filled with disbelief.

Maybe some hatred, too.

Even though Laurel had had some doubts that Theo was actually in love with her, she knew he had some feelings for her. In his own obsessed kind of way. However, she had also known that a one-sided relationship would never work.

Of course, now she was repeating that with Jericho.

Definitely one-sided. Yes, he'd kissed her several times, but that was just lust. There'd always be lust. But when he was thinking straight, and that would happen, he would remember that he would lose his family by being with her. Jericho wouldn't allow that to happen.

And neither would Laurel.

"There's a USB with an email conversation between Theo and a shrink named Dr. Marvin LaMastus," Levi relayed to them. He was still examining the envelope while volleying glances between it and them. "And there's also a statement from the nurse of the second psychiatrist. She says she never saw Laurel in the doctor's office, and there's no record of any appointment. Both the emails and the statement look legit."

"Of course they are," Theo snapped. "Both psychiatrists were pressured or bribed into giving their diagnoses."

"I don't suppose the shrink said anything in that email about Herschel hiring him?" Jericho asked.

Theo's jaw tightened even more. Maybe because they weren't jumping for joy over what he'd brought them. "You don't know what I had to do to contact Dr. LaMastus. I had to risk your father finding out."

"You poor thing." Jericho's voice was loaded with sarcasm. "Laurel was shot at. If you cared one ounce about her, you should be doing any and everything to help her get out of this mess."

Theo looked down at the wedding ring. "No. Not now. I'm done with her. As far as I'm concerned, you two deserve each other."

Normally, that would have been an insult, but considering Laurel had spent most of her adult life playing with the idea of marrying Jericho, she decided it wasn't much of an insult, after all.

Theo glanced at his mother before he stormed out the door.

But Dorothy didn't budge. She lifted her suddenly weary gaze to Laurel. "You have no idea what you've done."

Jericho glanced at Laurel to see if she knew what the woman was talking about. She didn't. Because this seemed to be a whole lot more than just a broken engagement, especially since Dorothy had never seemed that fond of her.

"Why don't you explain to me what I've done," Laurel insisted.

Dragging in a long breath, Dorothy got to her feet. "You need to annul this marriage and try to smooth things over with Theo. I'm not saying you have to go through with marrying my son, but you need to make it look as if you two have kissed and made up."

Was the woman insane? "Kiss and make up? Dorothy, someone's trying to kill Jericho and me. I'm on the verge of losing my son. My freedom. And you think all I have to do is kiss and make up with Theo?"

Dorothy nodded, and she must have worked her way through the shock of all of this because she suddenly looked a lot stronger. "I know you haven't forgotten about Rossman and Cawley. They'll kill you because of those failed business deals."

Laurel hated how those two, Rossman and Cawley, kept popping up, especially since no one had been able to find them. Was it really that simple—did the pair want her dead because of the money they'd lost from the broken business deals?

Because it felt like more than that.

"Do you have any proof whatsoever that Ross-man and Cawley hired someone to attack us?" Jericho asked. And yes, he was all lawman now.

"None." Dorothy didn't hesitate, either. "And you won't find anything, either. They're thorough, and they won't resurface until they've tied up every loose end in this mess."

Laurel was a loose end. Well, she was if she believed what Dorothy had said.

"You stand to lose a lot of money from those business deals, too," Laurel reminded the woman.

Dorothy stayed silent a moment. "Go ahead. If it makes you feel better, accuse me of this. But it won't help you. Nothing will, except your crawling back to Theo and begging for his forgiveness."

Laurel was just punchy enough to laugh. "That's not going to happen."

"Then I guess I'll be attending your funeral soon. Yours, too," Dorothy added to Jericho, and she walked out. Not in a hurry, either. More like a woman out for a Sunday stroll.

Jericho and she stood there, waiting until they saw Dorothy's limo drive away. Jericho holstered his gun, put his arm around her again, and it took Laurel a moment to realize why. She'd gone past the trembling stage, and her legs had nearly given way.

"I'm sorry," she said as tears watered her eyes.

Jericho cupped her chin, forced eye contact. "Not your doing."

"But it is. God, Jericho. I could cost you everything."

The anger flashed through his eyes. For just a moment, anyway. When their gazes connected again, there was a lot more than anger in them. There was a swirl of all the things that Laurel herself was feeling.

Including the heat.

Oh, yes. It was there, all right, thanks to that latest kissing session in his office. She had to do something to avoid kissing him again, and even as the thought flew through her head, Laurel knew there was zilch she could do about that. Jericho's lifted eyebrow let her know that he was right there on the same page with her.

Jericho's phone buzzed, and her heart skipped a beat or two when she saw Jax's name on the screen. Laurel held her breath, waiting and praying for good news.

"We made it to the safe house," Jax said when Jericho answered the call and put it on speaker. "We're all okay."

Once again, Laurel's legs turned wobbly—this time from sheer relief—and she leaned against Jericho to keep her balance. "Can I talk to Maddox?"

Even though you really couldn't have a phone

conversation with an eighteen-month-old, Jax didn't hesitate. "Tell Mommy hello," Jax instructed Maddox.

"Mama," Maddox said.

The warmth and the love went through her, head to toe. "Maddox, I love you."

And Jericho said the same thing to their son.

Maddox attempted to say it, as well, with love coming out as *wuv*. It was exactly what she needed to hear. Apparently, it worked for Jericho, too, because he smiled right along with her.

"Sorry, but he just spotted a toy chest," Jax said, coming back on the line. "Looks like he'll be busy for a while."

Laurel heard Maddox babble bye-bye.

She had no idea where this safe house was, but Laurel was glad it contained something to keep Maddox entertained. Glad, too, that he would have family with him. And that she'd gotten to hear his precious voice.

"We'll stay here until we hear from you," Jax added.

Heaven knew how long that would be, and it broke Laurel's heart to think she might not be able to spend Christmas with her son. Of course, that was the lesser of two evils. She didn't want Maddox to be in any danger.

"Is everything all right there?" Jax asked.

Definitely no smile from Jericho this time.

"Still working out some things. Thanks for everything, Jax." His gaze slashed to the front of the building. "Gotta go. I'll call you when I can."

Laurel tried to see what had caused Jericho's reaction, but as he had done with Dorothy and Theo, he pushed her behind him and drew his gun. Sweet heaven. Was there about to be another attack? Had those men in the SUV followed them here?

"What the hell is he doing here?" Jericho said under his breath.

However, she didn't have to see their visitor to know who it was. Because she soon heard his voice.

"Laurel," her father said, his voice syrupy sweet. "I thought I might find you here."

Chapter Twelve

Jericho's happy meter was at zero, and he was so not in the mood to deal with Laurel's father. Yet, here he was.

"You can wait in my office," Jericho said to Laurel. She didn't, of course. Not that he'd thought for one second that she would.

She was exhausted. Still unsteady on her feet. But Herschel's mere presence seemed to give him a jolt of energy and put some fire in her eyes.

"What do you want?" she snapped at her father. Definitely not a trace of affection.

Not that Jericho could blame her. Herschel was a snake of the worst kind. A man who'd destroy, or maybe even kill, his own child, to get what he wanted.

"You managed to delay the arrest warrants," Herschel said. "Clever. But not clever enough. Tomorrow morning, those warrants will be served."

"Predicting the future now? *Clever*," Jericho

repeated. "And please don't tell me you came all the way here to toss that puny threat at us."

"No." That's all he said for several moments. "A little bird told me Theo and Dorothy were just here." Herschel's gaze slid from Jericho and her to the papers that Levi was holding. "What did they give you?"

"Evidence to prove you're lying so you can frame Laurel," Jericho quickly answered.

There was a moment, just a moment, when there was some uncertainty in Herschel's body language, but it vanished, and he became the dirtbag father again.

"Whatever Theo gave you is a lie," Herschel insisted.

Jericho took a step toward the man. Hopefully, the look on his face was as mean-spirited as Jericho felt. "Oh, yeah? Why would Theo do that?"

"To cover his tracks, that's why. He's behind all of this."

"Really?" Laurel took a step closer to her father, too. "Theo has nothing to gain from having me committed to a mental hospital. Or nothing to gain from being tossed in jail. And he certainly has no solid reason to want me dead."

Herschel huffed. "Ever hear of revenge? Payback? Laurel, the man's obsessed with you. He'd rather see you dead than with someone else. Especially Jericho Crockett."

Theo was indeed obsessed. Furious, too, about the broken engagement. Add to that the money he had lost in the broken business deal with Rossman and Cawley, and yeah, that all added up to motive. But Herschel had the same motives. And more than that.

He wanted custody of his grandson.

"And you're obsessed with getting Maddox," Jericho spelled out for him. "Why, exactly? Is it to get back at Laurel? To put the screws to me? Or did you just wake up one morning and decide you wanted to be a bigger jackass than usual?"

Herschel had to do another quick wrestling match with his temper, but as he'd dealt with the surprise of Theo's evidence, he quickly corralled it. "I love Maddox. You know that."

"Do I?" Jericho asked. "Because you've said the words, but I'm just not feeling it. Maybe because you're not capable of love."

"I'm capable!" No corralling that time. Oh, boy. That was a little temper tantrum that Jericho was pleased to see. Pissed-off people usually said a lot more than calm ones. "And I don't want you or any Crockett raising my grandson."

There it was. In a nutshell. Despite the fact Herschel had almost certainly ordered Sherman Crockett's murder, it still wasn't enough. He wanted the rest of them to suffer, too.

And why?

All because Jericho's father had made it his business to put a stop to Herschel and his scummy dealings.

"I'm tired of talking to the two of you," Herschel grumbled. "And now I see you're married."

Jericho hadn't seen the man even glance at Laurel's wedding ring. Or maybe he'd heard the news from his *little bird* source. Probably some idiots he had spying on the sheriff's office.

"If you think a marriage will stop me from getting custody," Herschel added, "think again."

"The marriage alone might not," Jericho countered, "but I have a legal right to take custody of my son."

"Not if you're in jail. And I'll do anything to make sure you join my daughter behind bars. *Anything!*" Herschel took a huge risk by smiling, and Jericho had to do some temper corralling of his own so he didn't beat the man to a pulp.

"I'll add that threat to the evidence I have here," Levi said. He clicked off the tape recorder he was holding. There was no temper in his brother's voice. Just a calmness with the edge of the dark storm brewing beneath it.

Oh, Herschel didn't like that, either. "You can't just record me."

"Sure he can," Jericho argued. "This is an interview of a potential suspect. It's procedure to record it."

Levi nodded. Smiled, too. "I can turn it over to the Dallas PD so they know the real Herschel Tate." And as if it was a done deal, Levi picked up his phone.

Herschel volleyed some nasty glares among all three of them. "Trust me. You don't want to cross me."

Jericho went closer. Not quickly. He made sure Herschel heard each step. "Too late. The crossing's already been done. On my part. And yours." He leaned in, violating a lot of personal space. "Big mistake, Herschel. I *will* bring you down."

And it wasn't a bluff. Somehow, someway, Jericho would make it happen. Apparently, Jericho got his point across, because Herschel whirled around and left.

Jericho immediately turned to make sure Laurel was okay. She wasn't trembling, but he had no trouble seeing the worry in her eyes.

"This has to end," she said, her voice barely a whisper.

It wasn't a smart thing to do, but Jericho pulled her into his arms again. He was doing that a lot lately.

Wanting to do it, as well.

He didn't bother to curse the attraction. Or their situation. Hell, Laurel and he just seemed to end up together, no matter what.

"Let me make some calls, finish up a few

things here, get you something to eat," Jericho told her, turning her toward his office, "and I'll get you to another safe house. Not with Maddox," he added. "It's clear Herschel has someone watching the place, and it'd be too risky for you to go there."

She nodded. Blinked back tears. And just like that, she was back in his arms. Good grief. He hated seeing her put through the wringer like this. She was still in his arms, too, when Levi cleared his throat.

"I just got a call about Rossman and Cawley," his brother announced.

That got Laurel and Jericho moving apart, and they made their way to the desk Levi had been using. Levi put the call on speaker.

"This is Detective Mark Waters from the San Antonio PD on the line," Levi explained to them. "Mark, why don't you tell my brother what you just told me."

"Cawley's dead," Waters immediately explained. "He was killed in a car accident yesterday."

"Accident?" Jericho questioned. Because the timing of it sure was suspicious.

"That's what it's being called for now. Dallas PD is investigating since it happened in their jurisdiction. If they come up with anything, they said they'd call."

Jericho figured if Cawley had been murdered, there wouldn't be any evidence to find.

"What about Quinn Rossman?" Jericho pressed.

"Plenty of shady deals as Levi suspected, and the FBI's getting ready to arrest him for money laundering. I did find something interesting, though. Levi mentioned that Cawley and Rossman had lost a boatload of money from some failed business deals. One involving Laurel and Herschel Tate."

Beside him, Laurel pulled in her breath. Maybe because she thought this detective had found something else to incriminate her.

"Well, it turns out that Cawley and Rossman didn't lose a cent in those deals," Waters went on. "They moved what they'd planned to invest into something else and made a bundle. Turned out to be a very good thing for them. The only ones who lost money in that deal were Herschel, Theo James and his mother, Dorothy."

Bingo. That wasn't proof of which one was behind these attacks, but it did help Jericho narrow down his suspect pool from five to three.

"I need to talk to Rossman," Jericho insisted. "Even if it's a phone interview."

Because if he could get Rossman to admit that Laurel hadn't known anything about the money laundering, it could negate the charges against her. It would keep Laurel out of jail and go a long way to putting Herschel behind bars for orchestrating this.

"I'll see what I can do," Waters assured him.

Jericho thanked him and then stepped away when his phone buzzed. Laurel moved quickly to look at the screen. Probably because she thought it was from Jax. But it wasn't. The call was from his other brother, Chase. Since Chase was a marshal, Jericho hoped that something else hadn't gone wrong.

"I don't want any bad news," Jericho greeted him.

"Sorry."

Even without the sorry, Jericho knew something wasn't right. "Are you hurt?"

"Some. I'll be fine." But Chase's voice said otherwise.

"What the hell happened?" And a lot of bad possibilities started going through his head. Laurel's, too, since she gasped and pressed her fingers to her mouth.

"Jericho," Chase finally said, his voice sounding even weaker. "There's been a murder."

OH, MERCY.

The fear roared through her head like a piercing scream. "Maddox?" Laurel managed to say.

"Not Maddox," Chase answered. "This wasn't family."

That helped, but the fear already had her by

the throat, and Laurel couldn't just turn it off. Jericho put her in the chair next to the desk, turned down the volume on the speaker function of his phone and continued the conversation with Chase.

Levi stayed right there next to him, listening, no doubt to see if there was something they were going to have to buffer for her.

But Laurel didn't want a buffer.

If this murder had something to do with her or this situation she was in, she wanted to know. Too bad she could only hear snatches of the conversation, thanks to her own heartbeat throbbing in her ears. However, she did hear something that sent her pulse racing even more.

The Moonlight Strangler.

She prayed he didn't have anything to do with this. The man was a vicious serial killer. More than a dozen victims. And he was very good at murder, because he hadn't been caught in over thirty years. No one knew his name, but Laurel did know he was the biological father of Jericho's adopted sister, Addie.

He'd also murdered Jax's wife.

Had the Moonlight Strangler gone after Chase now?

His victims were usually young women, but maybe he'd made an exception.

"Read it to me," Jericho said to Chase.

Again, Laurel couldn't hear, but whatever Chase said to them had Levi and Jericho exchanging puzzled glances.

"Go ahead and get in the ambulance," Levi added, still talking to Chase. "I'll see if I can get there to check on you soon. When you can, tell one of the officers on the scene to fax us a copy of that note." He paused. "Hell, don't do that—

"He hung up," Levi said, adding some profanity. "Talk about being hardheaded. He's bleeding like a stuck pig, and he insisted on taking a picture of the note. Said he'll text it to you."

That had Jericho repeating Levi's *hell*.

Laurel wanted to curse, as well. What the devil was going on?

The moment Jericho finished the call, Laurel stood, faced him. "Is Chase all right?"

"I'm not sure," Jericho admitted. "The Moonlight Strangler clubbed him on the head and then knifed him in the chest. He's on his way to a San Antonio hospital right now."

This was bad. An injury like that could be fatal. "Levi, you'll need to go to him."

Levi nodded. "I will. After things are settled here."

She was about to remind him that might not happen, that he should be with his brother, but Jericho's phone dinged, indicating he had a message. Most likely from Chase.

"I'll get someone over to the bank," Levi told Jericho, and he stepped away to make a call, leaving Jericho to explain what the heck was going on.

"The Moonlight Strangler left a typed message on his latest victim's body," Jericho said. "It's about your father."

Of all the things she'd been expecting Jericho to say, that wasn't one of them. "My father? Why would the killer do that? And what did it say?"

Jericho shook his head. "I'm not exactly sure of the why part. Maybe because I'm Addie's brother, and he feels this warped family connection. Maybe he just hates your father as much as I do."

Laurel still didn't understand, but she got a better idea when Jericho handed her his phone so she could read the note for herself.

Doing you a little favor here, Sheriff Crockett. Not the dead body. Guess you wouldn't see that as a favor since you're one of the good guys. But you might want to hear a secret or two about the man who's after your honey and you. Herschel Tate. Funny, I got the label of a killer and he doesn't. Sometimes, the law doesn't have a long arm, after all, does it?

Laurel frantically scrolled down to read the rest. What would the Moonlight Strangler possibly know about her father?

She soon found out.

A little over thirty years, Herschel-boy was involved in a little gunrunning operation with me. You know all about it because you investigated it a couple of weeks ago.

Jericho had. Laurel knew all about it because it had been on the news. A man named Canales had tried to kill Addie because he'd been afraid she would remember he'd been involved in that gunrunning operation. An operation she might have witnessed as a child before being abandoned by her murdering birth father. But now, Canales was dead.

There are photos and such to prove Herschel was involved, Laurel read on. You can find that in a safe-deposit box rented to Wilbur Smith at the First National Bank over in Sweetwater Springs. Now, that's not my real name, so don't go off half-cocked. Just use what's in there to create a little justice for Herschel-boy. You're welcome, Sheriff Crockett.

Laurel read it again to make sure she hadn't misunderstood. "You really think there's proof?"

"We'll know soon," Levi answered. "I've got the bank manager and the Sweetwater Springs sheriff headed over there right now. The bank manager agreed to open the box because it could be connected to the Moonlight Strangler."

That was good since there could be other evidence in the safe-deposit box. But then she went through the details again. "A gunrunning operation over thirty years ago? The statute of limitations plays into this. My father can't be arrested for the crime even if there's proof."

"Unless he murdered someone," Jericho corrected. "No statute of limitations for that."

True. And the killer hadn't mentioned any proof of murder. Still... "Maybe if the evidence is strong enough, we can present it to a judge. It would go a long way toward preventing my father from getting custody of Maddox."

On its own, it wouldn't be enough, and they'd have to find a judge who wasn't in her father's pocket, but coupled with the info Theo had given them, then maybe they could use it to stop him.

Jericho glanced around as if trying to figure out what to do next. His gaze finally settled on Laurel. "I need to take you someplace safe so I can free up Levi to go check on Chase, and I'll get someone to cover the office. Don't tell Mom about any of this," he added to Levi. "Not until we know just how badly Chase is hurt."

Iris would no doubt be frantic once she heard about the attack, and she, too, would likely want to go to her son.

"With your mother gone, I'll need to be at the safe house with Maddox," Laurel insisted.

She expected Jericho to argue, to tell her that Jax and the two deputies could manage it. And they probably could. But Laurel wanted the three lawmen guarding her son to focus on protecting her son, not taking care of him.

"We have some time," Jericho finally said. "And if Chase's injury isn't that bad, we can keep the arrangement as is. If not, well, we'll just have to be careful when I take you there."

Part of Laurel was happy that she might soon be with Maddox again, but she didn't want Chase's injury to be so serious to make that happen. Plus, there was the risk of going to the safe house.

"Is it possible to find the people my father has watching us?" she asked.

Jericho went to the window, lifted one of the slats on the closed blinds and looked out, though he already knew what was out there.

Buildings. Lots of them.

Not just across the street but on each side of the sheriff's office. Her father's spy could be on the roof of one of those or maybe even inside. With long-range equipment, the spy could be anywhere on the street.

"Herschel probably has someone watching the roads, too." Jericho shook his head. "We could probably flush out someone nearby, but there's no telling how many people he hired."

True, and it wasn't as if her father was lacking for money.

Levi's phone rang, and he glanced at the screen. "Sheriff McKinnon from Sweetwater Springs." Thankfully, he put the call on speaker.

"It's here," the sheriff greeted. "Some old photos of what appears to be the sale and transfer of arms. There are also some notes with dates, names and such. And yes, Herschel Tate's name is included on them."

"But is he in the photos?" Levi asked.

"Hard to tell for sure, but it could be him. I'll have to send them to the lab, of course, but I'll fax you some copies."

"Thanks. I'm at the sheriff's office in Appaloosa Pass." Levi thanked him, ended the call and looked at his brother. "I'll wait here until you get someone to cover the office. It isn't a good idea to keep Laurel here much longer, though."

No. Because if her father's little bird told him about the contents of the safe-deposit box, then he might get desperate. There could be another attack.

Jericho nodded, took out his phone, but it buzzed before he could even make a call. Laurel figured it was an update on Chase.

It wasn't.

Quinn Rossman's name appeared on the phone screen.

"Sheriff Crockett," Rossman said the moment Jericho answered. "I understand you want to talk to me about Laurel and the money laundering charges against her. Well, let's talk. I'll be at the sheriff's office in just a few minutes."

Chapter Thirteen

Jericho felt as if he was being buried by an avalanche.

So much was coming at Laurel and him. Their impending arrests. The danger. Chase's injury. The new info from both Theo and the Moonlight Strangler.

Now, this.

Rossman would be arriving soon, and while Jericho did indeed want to have a chat with the man, he didn't want that to happen at Laurel's expense.

"What can I do to help?" Levi asked.

Jericho went with the most pressing problem—making sure Laurel was safe. "Call in the reserve deputies. I want at least two of them, and tell them to get here ASAP."

He used the computer to pull up the personnel roster for Levi. The deputies wouldn't be pleased about being called in since they were probably spending time with their families, but it couldn't be helped.

While Levi started to make the calls, Jericho turned to Laurel. Like him, she looked overwhelmed. Scared, as well. Too bad there was a reason to be scared. After all, Rossman hadn't been ruled out as a suspect, and with his partner, Cawley, now dead, Rossman could be looking to blame Laurel in some way for this mess they were all in.

"I know," she said before he could speak. "You want me to hide in your office. But until Rossman gets here, I can help."

Jericho was about to assure her that he had everything under control, but then he heard the whirring sound of the fax machine. No doubt, copies of the photos and notes from Sheriff McKinnon.

He tipped his head to the papers that the machine was spitting out. "Why don't you take those and go in my office."

She nodded, probably because she was interested in seeing if it was her father in the old photos, but she would also be safer in there than in the squad room. However, Laurel didn't jump to get the faxes. She stood there, staring at him.

"You'll be careful, right?" she asked.

"Yeah." But they both knew that being careful hadn't stopped the other attacks. It might not stop this one, either, if Rossman came in with guns blazing.

Since Jericho thought they both could use it, he brushed a kiss on her forehead. Then, her mouth. He could definitely be doing other things right now, but this seemed just as important as everything else.

"Go," he insisted before he kissed her again. "While I'm waiting for Rossman, I'll start to work on a place for us to stay."

Laurel finally got moving. She gathered up the papers and went to his office. "Don't open the window in there," he reminded her. Not that she would. "And just in case something happens, there's a gun in the center desk drawer."

Another nod, and he hated that Laurel barely had a reaction to being told about the gun. She was probably still partially in shock from the last attack because there was no way she could become immune to the possibility of someone trying to kill her again.

At least he hoped not.

No one should get used to that.

Jericho waited until she was inside his office before he took out his phone and went to one of the front windows to look out. He didn't raise the blinds. He looked out the side.

Since it was still butt-freezing cold, there weren't many people out and about, though there were several folks eating at the diner across the street. Jericho could also see cars pulling in and out of the parking lot of the grocery store just up the block. No one seemed to be focused on the sheriff's building. And there was definitely no sign of Rossman. Thankfully, Jericho had seen a photo of the man in the background report, so he should be able to recognize him.

Jericho made his call to a friend, Marshal Dallas Walker, and asked him to arrange a safe house. He had to add another ASAP to the request, and the marshal assured him he'd get right on it.

"The deputies are on their way," Levi relayed to him when he finished his calls. "What next?"

"Call and get an update on Chase. If it's good news, I'll phone Jax." He'd need to call Jax, anyway, to let him know what was going on, but Jericho preferred to have some good news before he did that.

Jericho returned to keeping watch. Still no sign of Rossman, but he heard Laurel step out of his office, and he pivoted in that direction. Considering all the bad stuff that'd been going on, he almost expected her to say they were under attack. Instead, she held up the handful of faxed photos.

"It's my father," she said. "Of course, he's a lot younger in the photos, but it's him, all right."

Good. The lab would still have to verify it, but this was a start. "What does it say about your father in the notes?" Jericho asked.

"He's mentioned in one of the deals to buy illegal weapons." Laurel blew out a frustrated breath. "But they're just notes. I can't imagine them being admissible in court."

They wouldn't be. But maybe the photos and notes together would be enough to get Herschel to back off. Jericho hated to bargain with the snake, but if Herschel thought he was fighting a losing battle to get Maddox, then maybe he'd call off his dogs.

Jericho motioned for her to go back in the office, and he made another sweeping glance of the street.

"Chase will be okay," Levi relayed while he was still on the phone. "He's got a concussion, and he'll need about a dozen stitches to the chest, but the cut isn't that deep. Once that's done, he should be able to leave the hospital."

That was even better news. Too bad getting the photos and notes had come at such a high price. A woman's murder and Chase's injury. Of course, the Moonlight Strangler had likely planned on murdering the woman, no matter what, but Jericho hated that the killer had done it this way.

"Chase said one of the Sweetwater Springs

deputies can bring Chase here to the sheriff's office," Levi added.

"Not here." Jericho didn't even have to think about that. "Tell Chase to go to the ranch." At least there were plenty of ranch hands who could help guard him, and their longtime cook had some decent nursing skills.

Jericho listened to Levi relay the message. Braced himself in case Chase argued about it.

But then something caught his attention.

A man in a dark, heavy coat was coming up the sidewalk across the street near the diner. No hat so Jericho got a good look at him. Dark hair, thin face.

It was Rossman.

Every nerve in Jericho's body went on alert.

"Rossman's here," he called out to Levi. "Laurel, don't come out."

"Is he armed?" Levi asked, joining Jericho at the window.

"Hard to tell." Jericho could see his hands, and Rossman wasn't carrying a gun, but that coat was big enough to conceal plenty of weapons.

Rossman turned his gaze toward the sheriff's office, and in the same motion, he caught onto the side of the diner. But he didn't just catch onto it. The man sank to his knees.

"What the hell?" Jericho went to the door,

opened it, and with his gun ready, tried to get a better look.

And he got one, all right.

A gust of wind flipped back the side of Rossman's coat, and Jericho saw the front of the man's shirt was bright red.

Blood.

"Call for an ambulance and cover me," Jericho said to Levi, and he stepped out, praying this wasn't some kind of ruse so that hired thugs could go after Laurel again.

Rossman lifted his head, made eye contact with Jericho. No ruse. Well, not on Rossman's part, anyway. The man was indeed hurt.

Maybe dying.

It was a risk. Anything he did at this point was. But Jericho kept watch around him and hurried across the street. Once he was closer, he saw there wasn't much color left in Rossman's face, and the man's breathing was thin and ragged.

"What happened to you?" Jericho asked, stooping down beside him. He tore open the shirt.

More blood.

Too much of it.

Rossman was bleeding out, and since the ambulance might not get there in time, Jericho held his hand against the gaping wound to try to staunch the blood.

"What happened?" Jericho repeated.

"I got shot." Rossman motioned up the street.

That's when Jericho saw a dark green car at the traffic light. The car's headlights and engine were still on, and the driver's-side door was wide-open. Someone had shot through the window, and the bullet had no doubt gone into Rossman.

Considering what'd happened to Rossman's business partner, Jericho figured the man had been followed and targeted.

Since the shooter could come back for another round, Jericho pulled the man into the narrow alleyway. A couple of the diners came outside, no doubt to see what was going on, but Jericho motioned for them to get back in.

"The ambulance will be here soon," Jericho told Rossman. "Just hold on a few more minutes."

"I don't have minutes. I'm dying." The hoarse breath he dragged in sure sounded like a man on his deathbed.

"Did you see the person who did this to you?" Jericho asked.

Rossman nodded, and his eyelids fluttered down. "He said I was to give her a message. Tell her that he's coming to kill her. To kill Laurel."

Well, hell. That was not a message Jericho wanted to hear. "Who's coming?" Jericho pressed.

"Herschel." That was all Rossman said for several long moments. "I didn't see him, but I heard his voice. He's the one who shot me."

Jericho got right in his face. "You're sure it was Herschel?"

But there was no way for Rossman to hear the question. No way for him to answer.

Because the man was already dead.

Chapter Fourteen

There was blood on her hands.

Not her own. And thankfully, not Jericho's. She wasn't exactly sure how it got there, but it belonged to Rossman.

After the ambulance had taken the man's body away and Jericho had come back into the sheriff's office, she'd ended up in Jericho's arms. Laurel was fuzzy about how that'd happened, too, but she'd pretty much lost it when he had told her what Rossman had said.

Of course, she'd known all along that her father was capable of murder. Had known he would do anything to get Maddox and get back at her. But now a man was dead, and he'd used his dying breath to deliver a message.

Tell her that he's coming to kill her.

There it was in a nutshell. So what if they had proof now to discredit her father and get the charges against her dismissed? That wouldn't matter if he was hell-bent on making sure she was dead.

And that riled her to the core.

Rossman's blood angered her, too, because it was yet another reminder of a life lost in this ordeal. Too many lives, including Jericho's father and her own mother. Added to that were the injuries and the fear that seemed to be crushing her lungs.

One way or another, Herschel was going to pay.

She heard the footsteps, and several moments later, Jericho appeared in the doorway of his office where she was waiting. He, too, still had blood on him and was sporting a very concerned expression. Something he'd had for the past hour, since Rossman had been murdered.

"Did you find my father?" she asked.

Some of the concern vanished, replaced by frustration when he shook his head. "Not yet. The deputies looked for him, but I brought them back in so the office—and you—would be protected. The Rangers just arrived so they'll take over the search."

If her father was indeed still out there, he was probably staying well hidden. Until it was time for the final attack against her.

"I'm making arrangements for a safe house," Jericho continued. "The Sweetwater Springs's sheriff has offered to lend me two of his deputies to do backup for us while we're at the safe house. But I'm also making this place as safe as possible in the meantime. We've got the security system turned on. And as I said, the reserve deputies are here. Levi, too. He's staying now that Chase doesn't need him."

She certainly hadn't forgotten about Chase, but with everything else going on, she'd pushed him to the back of her mind. "How's Chase?"

"He'll be okay. He's a Crockett, and along with a hard head, he's got thick skin like the rest of us."

Laurel appreciated Jericho's attempt to lighten things up, but nothing was going to work right now.

"Did you get a chance to call Jax?" Jericho asked her.

She nodded. "Everything's okay, but Maddox was asleep, so I didn't get a chance to talk to him. He doesn't usually go to sleep this early."

"Between the deputies, my mom and Jax, he's got four playmates. I'm betting they tired him out."

Maybe. She hoped that was true and that her little boy wasn't picking up on all the stress from the danger.

She certainly was.

Laurel felt wired and exhausted at the same

time. There was so much nervous energy bubbling up inside her and nowhere to aim it. Too bad her father wasn't around so she could give him a piece of her mind.

"Come on," Jericho said, helping her to her feet. "There's a bathroom just off the break room. Well, sort of a bathroom. No shower, but there's a sink. The water pressure's practically nonexistent, and the hot-water heater taps out after about a minute, but we can both wash off some of the blood."

Yes, they could wash it off, but Laurel would still see it.

Still feel it, too.

"Laurel's going to get some rest," Jericho told Levi when he leaned around the hall corner to look into the squad room.

His brother was obviously busy, but Levi muttered something about that being a good idea. And it was, in theory. But that didn't mean it was going to happen. Not with her mind in tornado mode.

"I wish my father was dead," she said.

Jericho made a quick sound of agreement and led her toward the break room. A place she already knew too well since she'd stayed there for hours the night after the first attack. Maddox had slept on the small bed tucked against the wall while she paced and worried about, well, everything. She wasn't pacing now, but the worry was still there in spades.

He opened one of the metal lockers positioned against the wall and took out a gray T-shirt. He held it up, glancing at it, then at her.

Jericho tossed her the T-shirt. "It won't be a good fit, but it'll be better than nothing."

It would be. She didn't want any more reminders of the violence that'd just taken place.

The blinds were still closed, and he slapped off the overhead lights. However, it didn't plunge them into total darkness because of the light coming from the hall. There were also lights threading in around the edges of the blinds. Plenty of light for her to see the worried look on his face.

"Is there something you aren't telling me?"

He looked down at the blood on her hands. On the front of her top, too. "I just don't like seeing that on you."

"I could say the same thing." She touched the front of his shirt. Of course, that meant she touched his chest, too. Not a good idea, considering her raw nerves and spiked adrenaline.

Also not a good idea because of the attraction.

Jericho didn't exactly step back, but it was close. He glanced away, dodging her gaze and dodging her touch in the process. Wise decision. His mind was likely in tornado mode, too.

"Go ahead. Wash up," he said, opening the bathroom door for her.

Laurel didn't turn on the light, and since there was no window, there was even less light in here than in the break room itself. Still, she found her way to the sink and began to wash off the blood.

"My father took a huge risk by shooting Rossman," Laurel said, thinking out loud. Thinking quietly about it, too. There was something about this that just didn't add up.

Jericho made a sound of agreement, but she could still see his face, and that wasn't agreement in his expression. "Think this through. Pulling the trigger himself just isn't something Herschel would do. So, why do it now? Especially when he has his spies planted all around. Why not just get one of them to do his dirty work?"

Good question. Too bad Laurel didn't have a good answer. "You think Rossman would use his dying breath to lie?"

"He might if he was dying, anyway, and wanted to get back at Herschel. Heck, Rossman could have even shot himself. A suicide so he could incriminate your father. After all, Rossman was about to be arrested for money laundering. His partner's already dead, so he might have figured this was the easy way out."

She splashed some water on her face while she thought about that. Yes, a suicide was possible. But it was also possible that either Theo, Dorothy or both had ordered the hit on Rossman.

Laurel groped around until she located a towel. Dried her face. And then debated how to change out shirts. She didn't especially want to close the door between Jericho and herself, but it probably wasn't a good idea to strip down in front of him, either, so she stepped back into the corner of the bathroom to change. When she came back out, she realized he was staring at her.

Judging from the heat in his eyes, maybe she hadn't been in the shadows as much as she thought. Best not to bring it up, though. And it wasn't as if they didn't have anything else to think about. Or talk about.

"My father has a strong motive for wanting Rossman dead," she reminded him. Reminded herself, too.

Jericho nodded. "But it still doesn't feel right. Herschel would have found another way. Maybe a car accident like the one that Rossman's partner had. Now, that's something Herschel would do."

"But Rossman said he saw my father."

"He could have lied about that. Or maybe he did see him. Herschel's probably still in town somewhere, and Rossman could have been at the wrong place at the wrong time."

Or else someone could have made sure he was there by luring him to the area. Theo or Dorothy could have certainly managed that. And that meant they were back to square one again.

Well, almost.

"You can still use Rossman's accusation to arrest my father." Her father might be able to wiggle out of the charges, but that would take time, and it would give him something else to focus on rather than Jericho and her.

"Oh, yeah," Jericho quickly agreed. "And trust me, that's exactly what'll happen when he's found. I've asked the Rangers to assist in the search."

Good. So, not square one.

"But we need more," he added. "I'm playing around with the notion of trying to set some kind of trap to lure your father or anyone else involved in this."

"What kind of trap?"

He shook his head. "Not sure yet. I'm still trying to work it all out. But once I have the details set in my mind, you'll be the first to know."

Jericho peeled off his blood-stained shirt and headed into the bathroom. As she'd done, he scrubbed his hands, hard. His face, too. But since she was holding the only towel, he came back into the doorway to take it from her.

"You're worrying," he pointed out, frowning. Maybe because she was frowning at herself. "You shouldn't. There's good news in all of this.

With Herschel arrested and charged with murder, that'll make it easier to ax the arrest warrants against both of us. Ax his custody petition, too."

Laurel heard every word he said. Felt the relief that the danger might finally be ending. But she also had a shirtless Jericho standing in front of her, and he hadn't even attempted to find a shadowy corner to hide while he dried off.

She saw it then. The faint scar on his chest where her name had once been.

"What?" he asked. But then he scowled when he followed her gaze. "Yeah, I had it removed."

That was to be expected. But Laurel couldn't help remembering the time he'd first gotten it when they were still teenagers. A tattoo to prove to her that she'd always be part of him.

As if she needed ink to prove that.

If there was a test for it, she was sure Jericho was in her veins, in her blood. He was certainly in her heart.

"What can I say? I was young, and in those days words alone didn't seem to be a strong enough man-statement." He walked past her, heading toward the locker again. No doubt for another shirt. But he didn't take out anything. He just stared inside the locker as if expecting to find some kind of answer there.

"It was a statement. I remember you trying to pretend it didn't hurt like crazy. The tattoo," she clarified when he turned around to face her again.

Still no shirt. Just that intense stare that only Jericho could manage. "It hurt," he verified.

And they were no longer talking about the tattoo.

She shouldn't touch him. Laurel knew that. Touching Jericho was never as simple as just touching, and it could be dangerous.

It didn't stop her.

As if her hand had a mind of its own, it went to his chest, and the moment she felt him beneath her fingers, the relief came. Washing over her. Through her. For this brief time, she hadn't lost him. He was still hers to touch.

Hers to take.

Of course, it was pure fantasy. He was no one's for the taking, especially hers, but when it came to Jericho, she'd spent most of her life weaving fantasies, and tonight was apparently no different.

He glanced at her hand. "You plan on doing something about that?" Those sizzling amber eyes came back to hers and held. Waiting.

Without lifting her hand, Laurel inched it lower. To his stomach. She hadn't thought she could ache more for him, but she'd been wrong. Every part of her was aching now. Every part wanting him. Wanting more. She was so close to his zipper. Close enough that she could *do something about that*.

Something she was sure they'd regret when they came to their senses.

But not now.

No regrets now.

She leaned in to kiss him, but Jericho beat her to it. His rough hand went around the back of her neck and dragged her closer. Not for a kiss, though. He just stared at her, studying her. So much emotion in his face. A tangled mix that Laurel was feeling, too.

"Damn you," he growled. He shut the door. Locked it.

And he kissed her.

Laurel had wanted that kiss more than her next breath, but she still wasn't ready for it. Jericho mouth's came to hers, and she remembered that he kissed with the same intensity that he did everything else in his life. No gentle lead-in. Just the sweet assault of his taste and his body against hers.

He took her hand, put it over the front of his jeans. "Are you going to do something about that?" he demanded.

She did. Laurel unzipped him, slowly, eased her hand into his jeans and beneath his boxers. And she got the reaction she wanted. Not only was he hard as stone, he made a sound, deep in his chest.

Before he dragged her to the bed.

It was exactly what Laurel wanted. This fire. This need that only Jericho could fix. And he fixed, it all right.

Everything was urgent. Fast. As if this had become a life-and-death matter. He stripped off her borrowed T-shirt. Her bra, too. And Laurel got the full impact of having his bare skin against hers. It didn't rob her of her breath exactly, but Jericho did something else to make sure that happened.

As she'd done with him, he slipped his hands into her jeans, into her panties, touching her while slipping off her jeans at the same time. Laurel wanted to help him. She freed him from his boxers but wanted to get rid of any and all barriers between them. His touch stopped her from doing that.

No ordinary touch.

No.

His fingers went inside her, and just like that she went from being on fire to being very close to climaxing. Something she didn't want to happen. Not until he was inside her, anyway.

Laurel tried to distract him with a kiss. Tried to get off his jeans, too. But Jericho kept on touching her, his fingers sliding in and out of her. Until she couldn't hold on any longer.

In the milky light, their gazes met. Held. And he sent her flying right over the edge.

Even as the pleasure wracked her body, she cursed him. "I wanted us to do this together."

"We will." It almost sounded like a threat.

Laurel wasn't sure if she should laugh or be worried. But she didn't have time for either. He rid her of her panties. Didn't bother with his jeans, though. Maybe because the need was too urgent. He kneed her legs apart and robbed her of her breath again when he pushed inside her.

The pleasure was blinding.

Not that she'd expected anything less.

The earlier climax now felt like foreplay. Jericho's version of foreplay, anyway. This was the real deal. The avalanche of emotions and pleasure that only he could give her. No pleasure on his face, though. Just the intensity to finish this.

To finish her. Again.

And he would. He always did.

Her body knew this rhythm they created together. Knew just how to move with him.

Or so she thought.

But Jericho made a move inside her that robbed her of what little breath she had left. It fueled the urgency for both of them. Turned his need-laced battle into an out-and-out war.

With their gazes still locked, Jericho pushed into her. Faster. Harder. Deeper. And even when her vision started to blur again, Jericho caught onto her chin, forcing her to hold the eye contact.

As if he'd rehearsed every moment, every move, he pushed into her one last time. The climax came. Even stronger than the last one. It came for him, too. Laurel felt his body surrender. And heard the single word he said loud and clear even though it barely had any sound.

"Hell."

Chapter Fifteen

Jericho gave himself a minute to let the feeling of release slide through him. It was a darn good minute, too, what with the intense pleasure and the feel of a naked Laurel beneath him. But he'd known right from the start that the minute and the pleasure couldn't last.

Time to deal with some reality.

Especially since reality was staring him right in the face.

Laurel's eyes were still a little glazed. His probably were, too. Great sex could do that, and there was no doubt about it. It'd been great. Always was when he was with Laurel. But great didn't mean there wouldn't be some serious consequences.

"Hell?" she said, repeating what he'd just gutted out.

"I didn't mean it like that."

Jericho rolled off her, damn near fell on his butt because the bed was so narrow. The jolt of having to keep his balance caused the last after-shocks of pleasure to vanish.

It wouldn't be long though before the need for her returned.

Always did.

"Then how did you mean it?" she asked. Laurel got up when he did, and she started to dress. It was a shame. Because the view of her naked was amazing.

Hard to give her a flat look when her breasts were still bare. She quickly did something about that and put her bra back on.

"You know what I mean," he insisted. "This complicates things."

She nodded. Sighed. And then she put on her jeans and the peep show was over. "Because your family will never accept me. Because *you'll* never accept me."

Jericho's flat look turned to a scowl. And because that last part riled him, he hooked his hand around the back of her neck and kissed the living daylights out of her.

"Trust me, I've *accepted* you," he snarled. And gotten himself worked up again in the process.

Laurel's mouth twitched. Maybe from the hard kiss. Maybe because she was fighting back a smile. Since she was a smart woman, she won. The smile didn't.

"Just so you know. I haven't been with anyone else since that last time with you," she added.

The night he'd gotten her pregnant. The reminder hit him like a punch. "I didn't use a condom." A first. Oh, man. He was clearly losing it. "I don't guess you're on the pill?"

She shook her head and didn't look nearly as alarmed as he did. "No need for it. Well, not until tonight, anyway. It's okay. It's the wrong time of the month."

Maybe. But considering he'd used a condom the last time and Laurel had still gotten pregnant, then maybe there was no *wrong time of the month* when it came to the two of them.

"At least we're married," he said, because he had no idea what else to say.

Now her smile won out. Jericho didn't join in on it.

"You're a serious distraction, you know that?" He dropped another kiss on her smiling mouth and unlocked the break room door so he could go and do all the things he should have been doing instead of having sex with Laurel.

Too bad he couldn't say it wouldn't happen again. And soon.

Yeah, he was losing it, all right.

"Good news," Levi said the moment Jericho glanced into his office, where Levi was working at the desk. A place Jericho should be. "We got a warrant for Herschel's arrest for Rossman's murder."

That was indeed good news. Jericho needed a whole lot more, though. Because as long as Herschel and those hired guns were at large, the danger would still be there for Laurel and Maddox.

"And the FBI got a match to Herschel's voice on the recording from those surveillance tapes involving the money laundering," his brother added. "There'll be a warrant coming for that, too."

Levi glanced at him. Did a double take. Then stared at Jericho—specifically at Jericho's rumpled clothes and not-quite-right expression.

"Want to talk?" Levi asked him.

"Not about *that.*" Jericho huffed. "Why, do you want to tell me how wrong it is to get involved with Laurel again?"

"No."

All right. That was a surprise. "Then what do you want to tell me?"

"That you're human."

Jericho huffed. "What the hell is that supposed to mean?"

"It means you and Laurel have skirted this attraction for years. Fighting it. Giving in to it. Cursing yourself. Did you curse her, too?"

Yeah, in an indirect way he had. He'd said that

hell. No plans to admit it, either. "Is there a point to all of this?"

"There is. If you two decide to quit skirting, then the family will eventually accept it. Hear me out," Levi added when Jericho was about to argue with that. "Laurel and you have a child. That'll bring Mom around. She's already said she wants a truce with Laurel, and I believe she means it."

But that was only one piece of this messy puzzle. "What about Herschel killing Dad?"

"What about it? True, Herschel almost certainly did kill him. But there's never been an ounce of proof that Laurel had any part in it either before or after the fact."

"But I knew," Jericho heard Laurel say, and he cursed himself for not hearing her walk up behind them. In addition to his mind, his ears were going, too. "I didn't have any proof, but I knew he'd done it."

"And without proof, there wasn't a damn thing you could do about it," Levi reminded her. Something that Jericho should have been telling her.

Laurel shook her head. "Still, I stayed under his roof. I continued to work for him."

Levi jumped right on that, too. "Because of your sick mother. I get that. I'd do the same if it were my mother."

Jericho scowled at Levi. It was the right thing

to say. Right time to say it, too. But those right words should have been coming from Jericho's mouth.

"All right." Levi held up his hands. Obviously, Levi hadn't missed Jericho's sharp look. "Then you tell her. And this time try it without scowling. Without cursing."

It got so quiet in the room that he could have heard an eyelash fall, and it took Jericho a lot longer to gather his thoughts.

Too long.

Because Laurel leaned in and kissed him. Hard. "It's okay. We'll work it all out later. For now, we'll work on keeping Maddox safe. Christmas is only a matter of hours away, and I'd like for us to spend that day with him. With all of us safe."

Well, hell's bells. Now she was saying the right thing, too. And she was right.

"You said something earlier about possibly setting a trap," she added.

"What kind of trap?" Levi immediately asked.

One that could out and out fail. Still, Jericho hadn't been able to come up with anything else to bring the danger to a quick end. Laurel was right. Time was ticking away.

Jericho made sure they didn't have any visitors in the squad room just in case Herschel had sent in one of his spies pretending to need some kind of help. But the only people out there were the two reserve deputies who were both busy working.

"Earlier, while the deputies were looking for Herschel, I spoke to Sheriff McKinnon over in Sweetwater Springs about possibly leaking some false information." Jericho hoped this made sense when he said it aloud. "Information about what was in the message that the Moonlight Strangler left at the crime scene."

Laurel shook her head. "What kind of false information?"

"The press has made a big deal out of the fact that the Moonlight Strangler hasn't gone after Addie. Or anyone else in the family since they found out that she's his daughter. I've seen some reporter speculate that the serial killer is actually helping us on cases."

Jericho wanted to put that speculation to good use.

"I want it leaked that the Moonlight Strangler has evidence that could prove who's been trying to kill Laurel. Evidence he intends to send to the cops tonight." Jericho continued, "It'd have to be something specific."

"Like proof of payment to the hired guns," Levi supplied. "Or photos of the person meeting with one of the men."

"Exactly like that. Something that could be used to trace the thugs back to the person who hired them. And it'll help that it's probably already leaked that the killer left something on his latest victim's body. We could say that a courier will bring the evidence to the Sweetwater Springs's sheriff office tonight, where it'll be prepped to be sent to the crime lab."

Another headshake from Laurel. "But what if the person who wants me dead goes after the sheriff and deputies in Sweetwater Springs? Or what if he goes after the courier?"

"The courier will be guarded, and Sheriff McKinnon will be ready for an attack." At least that's what McKinnon had assured Jericho. He hoped that was true because he didn't want this to turn out badly for the fellow sheriff who was trying to do them a huge favor.

"It might not work," Jericho added. "The person responsible could see right through the ruse and attack us here or while we're on the way to the safe house. We have to be ready for that."

More silence. But this time it didn't last very long, and Laurel nodded. "Let's do it. Anything to put an end to this."

Levi stayed quiet a moment longer. Then nodded. "I'm in."

Jericho added his own nod and took out his

phone to call Sheriff McKinnon. He just hoped like the devil that this was the right thing to do.

And that he wasn't about to set another attack in motion.

THERE WAS NOTHING to do but wait. Something Laurel had been doing for the past two hours. She just wasn't good at it, especially when lives were on the line to save Maddox and her.

She was tired of the danger. Tired of hiding. Tired of being away from her son. And especially tired of people dying because of some stupid plan that'd been set in motion by her father. Maybe by Theo or Dorothy. They might soon know if the trap that Jericho set worked.

The sheriff's office was quiet. For a change. The two deputies were keeping watch at the back of the building. Jericho and Levi were at the front. Laurel was in Jericho's office, away from the wall of front windows. It would be a gutsy move for someone to attack a building with four cops inside, but the other attacks had been gutsy, as well. Added to that, the person might be as desperate as Laurel was to put an end to all of this.

She leaned back in the chair, tried to settle her nerves. No chance of that happening, so she used one of the secure phones to call Jax. But it wasn't Jax who answered. It was Iris.

Laurel's heart went straight to her throat. "Is something wrong? Why didn't Jax answer?"

"Everything's fine. Jax is eating, that's all, and when I saw the number on the screen, I thought it might be you calling. Maddox is still sleeping," Iris went on. "I think he got tired out from all the ride-the-horsey games he played with Jax. Maddox is such a sweet little boy, Laurel."

"Yes, he is. Thank you."

"You're welcome. And I should have said it sooner. I should have said a lot of things sooner." Iris paused. "Like welcoming you to the family since Jericho and you are married now."

"I'm not sure how long that'll last." The moment Laurel heard her own words, she winced. "I mean, you know he only married me so he could keep my father from getting custody of Maddox. But it looks as if my father won't stand a chance at doing that now."

"Yes, Jax told me about that. It'll be an answer to a lot of prayers if Herschel is stopped." Another pause. "But that doesn't have anything to do with Jericho and you and your marriage. You two have always been together, even when you weren't. And you're good together."

Laurel got a flash of a naked Jericho with her in the break room, and despite everything else, she felt a trace of pleasure ripple through her again.

"I guess what I'm saying is I won't stand in the way of making this marriage permanent," Iris continued. "In fact, I think you should make it permanent."

Laurel certainly hadn't seen that coming. "You mean for Maddox's sake."

"No. For you and Jericho. Just think about it."

She was about to assure Iris that she would. She was about to thank her, as well, but Laurel heard Jericho and Levi talking in the squad room. Their voices weren't raised or frantic, but there was something in Jericho's tone that put Laurel on full alert.

"I need to go," she said to Iris. "I'll call you back."

Laurel clicked the end call button and went to the doorway so she could see Jericho and Levi. Levi was on the phone, but Jericho immediately turned to her. Yes, she could tell from the look on his face that something had indeed happened.

"Your father was spotted in town," Jericho said. "Just a couple of blocks from here."

All right. That required her to take a deep breath. Of course, she'd known he was nearby. Well, he was if Rossman had been telling the truth, that is.

"I'd faxed your father's picture to all the businesses that were still open, and the security guard at a storage facility spotted him a couple of minutes ago. Not alone. There were two other men in the car with him."

Hired guns no doubt. "Is he coming here?" she asked.

"Maybe." But his expression said *definitely.* She was the reason her father had come here, and his spies had likely already told him exactly where she was.

Laurel wasn't afraid. She was well past that point when it came to her father. It was pure anger now. In fact, if she knew that Jericho and the others wouldn't be hurt, she would demand a showdown with him.

But maybe there was something she could do.

"I'm calling my father," she said, and Laurel didn't wait for permission from Jericho. Something he'd never give her, anyway.

"Laurel," Jericho snapped, his voice a stern warning.

However, she had already pressed in the number, and when her father answered on the first ring, she put the call on speaker.

"Jericho?" Her father's greeting was as frosty as Jericho's glare. The one he was volleying between the phone and her.

"No, it's me," Laurel said. "I understand you're in town. Are you coming to see me?"

"Right. As if I'd let you know where I am or

where I'm going. You'd just tell Jericho, and he'd arrest me. Or kill me."

"Jericho's not a killer. But you are."

Her father cursed, and like Jericho's glare, some of it was aimed at her. "I didn't kill Rossman."

"That's not what he said," Laurel argued.

"Well, he was mistaken. I was there, yes, because I got a call from one of my men. He said there was something I needed to see. Turned out to be a trap. Somebody shot Rossman, and now I'm getting the blame."

That was possible, for her father to have been set up, but it was just as possible that he was lying.

"Rossman isn't the only death connected to you," she said.

"Ah, now we're talking about Sherman Crockett. Since I suspect your *husband* is listening to our every word, then that's one topic that's not up for discussion."

Jericho opened his mouth, no doubt to return verbal fire, but Laurel lifted her hand, motioned for him to stay quiet. Yes, her father probably did know that Jericho would be there with her, but she figured she would get more information out of him than Jericho would.

Well, maybe.

At the moment her father probably hated her

more than he hated Jericho, and she might be able to strike a nerve. One that would get him to blurt out a confession.

"First Sherman, then my mother," Laurel said.

Silence. For a long time. "Your mother was dying."

"Possibly. Did you help that process along by giving her an overdose of painkillers?"

More silence. "She was in a lot of pain. No matter what you think of me, I loved her in my own way. I couldn't stand to see her suffering."

It took her a moment to rein in her own temper just so she could speak. "You didn't love her. And she didn't love you. She was terrified of you, and so help me, you'll pay for killing her."

"I didn't kill her!" he shouted. "What, are you recording this? You think you can use it against me?"

"There's already enough evidence against you. And there's already a warrant out for your arrest."

"A warrant, yes," her father agreed, "but they'll have to find me to serve it. In the meantime, I've got my entire legal team working to clear my name. And it will be cleared... What the hell..."

Laurel was about to ask him why he'd said that, but Jericho's phone buzzed. He glanced at the screen and immediately stepped away and answered it.

Laurel hurried after Jericho. "What's wrong?"

Jericho was already talking to the person on the other end of the line, but he paused to answer her. "Someone just fired shots into the Sweetwater Springs sheriff's office."

Chapter Sixteen

So, someone had taken the bait.

Jericho was partially happy about that, but he darn sure wasn't pleased that Sheriff McKinnon and his deputies were under fire.

"Are they okay?" Laurel asked. The color had drained from her face.

He considered going with a lie so that maybe he could ease some of the fear in her eyes, but Laurel was right in the thick of this with him. "I don't know," Jericho answered honestly. "Sheriff McKinnon only had a few seconds to tell me what was happening. I heard shots in the background," he added.

She nodded. And, yep, the fear stayed. "What if they don't capture one of their attackers alive?"

"They will." Okay, that was possibly a lie, one that Jericho had to believe. If they didn't or if they couldn't get the hired gun to talk, then all of this danger had been for nothing.

Well, except for the fact that if the hired guns

were there in Sweetwater Springs, they weren't anywhere near the safe house that contained Maddox. Jericho hated to put fellow lawmen's lives on the line, but if their situations were reversed, Jericho would have done the same for them.

Jericho went back to the window to keep watch, but he also tipped his head to the phone she was holding. "Is your father still on the line?"

She shook her head. "He hung up."

That was just as well. Herschel had come darn close to incriminating himself, but he was too clever to spill anything important. Especially anything that would get him the death penalty. Of course, he might not have to spill anything if they could get the murder charges to stick. Or if Sheriff McKinnon managed to get a confession from the thugs who were now shooting at him.

"Is anyone out there?" Laurel asked. Still too pale, and he was pretty sure she was trembling now. Jericho wanted to go to her, but the shooting at Sweetwater Springs could be a ruse to get them to lower their guard.

Wasn't going to happen.

"You should go back in my office," he insisted. Fewer windows there. "Make sure you leave the light on."

That was a departure from what he usually told her, but Jericho had turned on every light in the place. Including the bathroom. He hoped that way, if hit men did show up, they wouldn't know what room Laurel was in. Plus, the interior lights helped illuminate the front sidewalk and the sides of the building.

"Be careful," Laurel said.

Jericho glanced back at her, their gazes connecting. Usually when that happened, he felt a punch of heat from the attraction, but now he saw something else.

Something he didn't like.

"I'm not going to get shot," he let her know. Possibly another lie, but there was no need for her to be worried about him.

"See anything?" Jericho asked Levi once Laurel was back in his office.

"No. You?"

"Nothing." Jericho reminded himself that was a good thing, but he still had a knot in his gut. A knot that tightened when his phone buzzed, and he saw the caller's name.

Theo.

Jericho didn't want to tie up his hands for the call, so he hit the answer button, sandwiched the phone between his shoulder and ear. "Make it quick," Jericho snarled. "I'm busy."

Plus, Theo could be calling to try to distract him, which meant Jericho didn't care to have a long chat.

"Is Laurel okay?" Theo asked.

That didn't help his uneasiness, and Jericho made another sweeping glance of the area around the building. "Why do you ask?"

"Because she's in danger, that's why. Hell, we're all in danger."

"Some of us more than others," Jericho remarked. "Unless you've got something new and interesting to tell me—like a confession—then this call is over."

"Don't hang up!" It wasn't a shout. More like a plea. But it took Theo a few seconds to continue. "I think someone wants me dead."

"That's not a confession. Heck, it's not even a surprise. You piss people off, Theo. Me included."

"But you didn't just try to kidnap me. Did you?"

"No. That wasn't on my to-do list tonight." Now it was Jericho's turn to pause. "First, did this so-called kidnapping attempt really happen? And if so, did it happen in my jurisdiction?" Because if it didn't, then that was yet another reason to end the call and have him whine to somebody else.

"It happened just a few minutes ago. I'm a couple of streets away from the sheriff's office near the hotel. Two big guys jumped out of a black car when I was at the traffic light, and they tried to Taser me. I got away."

"Convenient." And possibly the truth. Because it could be true, Jericho had to use his lawman's voice. "Were you hurt?"

"Just some scrapes and bruises. I carry a concealed .38. Yes, I have a permit," he added before Jericho could ask. "Anyway, I managed to draw it, and I think I hit one of them when I fired."

Hell. Discharge of a weapon. Possible injury along with a possible kidnapping attempt. It would have to be investigated, but this was one duty Jericho would have to delegate.

"Call the Rangers," Jericho told Levi. "Tell them there's a situation I need them to handle at the Saltgrass Inn."

"You're not coming to help me?" Theo asked. Clearly, the man had heard what Jericho had said to his brother.

No way. Jericho had no intention of leaving Laurel to walk into what could be a trap or a ploy to get him away from Laurel. "Why are you here in town?"

"I got a call from one of your deputies who told me Laurel was in trouble, that I needed to go to the sheriff's office and check on her because she wanted to see me."

Theo hadn't hesitated, which meant it could be the truth or he could have just practiced the lie until it rolled right off his tongue. "Laurel doesn't want to see you, and no deputy of mine called you."

"But he did. He said his name was Mack Parkman—"

"Was his name on the caller-ID screen?" Jericho snapped.

"No. It said unknown number. But I figured your deputies were just using secure cells."

Mack was, since he was at the safe house with Jax and Maddox, but there would have been no reason for Mack to call Theo. Still, the lawman in him had to rule it out. Jericho jotted down a note for Levi to call Mack and verify that he'd had no phone contact with Theo.

"I want to come to the sheriff's office and see Laurel," Theo started up again. "And don't say she's not there, because she'll be wherever you are."

"Don't be so sure of that."

"I need to talk to her," Theo said, not even addressing Jericho's comment.

"Mack didn't call him," Levi whispered to Jericho.

Just as Jericho had figured. And yes, he trusted Mack, had known him his entire life. Theo, however, had reason to lie—so he could try to worm his way in and see Laurel. And if he wasn't lying, then someone like Herschel or

Dorothy could have hired anyone to make the call to lure Theo out so he could be kidnapped.

And there's where Jericho's theory came to a sudden stop.

Would Dorothy really try to hurt her own son?

Probably, if she blamed Theo for blowing the engagement with Laurel. That broken engagement had cost Dorothy a bundle. Then there was also the possibility that she hadn't wanted to hurt Theo but rather had wanted to set up someone to make it look as if they had murder or kidnapping on their mind.

Someone like Herschel.

Because if Dorothy was riled at Theo for losing those big bucks, she might aim the same venom at Herschel.

Or vice versa.

Herschel definitely wasn't a saint.

"Well, can I see Laurel?" Theo pressed.

Jericho was about to tell him a loud no, with some curse words added to it. But he didn't get the chance to say anything.

Because a blast shook the entire building.

THE SOUND WAS DEAFENING, and Laurel caught on to the wall to steady herself. Not a gunshot. This was something much bigger and louder.

What the heck had Theo done now?

She'd known that Jericho was talking to him,

but from what she could hear, it didn't seem as if he'd been threatening Jericho. However, something had definitely happened.

Laurel didn't bolt from the office, but she peered out the door. Jericho was still at the window where she'd last seen him. One of the blinds had fallen to the floor, and she could see the fireball in the street directly in front of the sheriff's office.

"Stay back," Jericho warned her. "It was a bomb."

Her heart was already pounding, but that news made it worse. "How did Theo get close enough to use a bomb?"

"I'm not sure it was Theo. I think someone on the roof of the diner tossed it down."

Oh, mercy. That meant they could have been aiming for the building itself. It also might mean this bomb wasn't the only one they had.

"Get under my desk," Jericho added.

"You should, too." Though she knew it wouldn't do any good.

Jericho just shook his head. "Go!"

Laurel did as he said. She scrambled under his desk just as she heard another sound. Not the blast from a second bomb.

But rather a gunshot.

Then, another.

She couldn't be sure, but Laurel thought maybe

they'd been fired into one of the front windows. The glass was bullet resistant, she remembered Jericho saying that, but it didn't mean the shots couldn't eventually get through. She prayed that Jericho and Levi were staying down.

"The shots stopped at the Sweetwater Springs office," Levi relayed to Jericho. "No one was hurt, and the shooters ran off."

That was good. The lawmen there were no longer under attack, but it was clear the shots hadn't stopped here. Because she heard several more of them crack into the windows.

Laurel gasped when another sound shot through the room. Since she was already bracing herself for the worst, it took her a moment to realize it was a landline phone on Jericho's desk. She wasn't sure if she should answer it or not, but when it kept ringing, Laurel thought it might be someone calling to report a sighting of their attacker. She grabbed the phone and got back under the desk.

"Who is this?" the caller immediately asked.

Laurel groaned. Because it was Dorothy on the line. "It's me. And I don't have time to talk."

"Then, make time," the woman insisted. "Because what I have to tell you could save your life."

All right. That grabbed her attention. "What do you mean?"

"I mean, Theo has gone stark raving mad, that's what. He's trying to get to you so he can kill you. And he's trying to do the same thing to me. Don't trust him, Laurel."

"I won't. I won't trust you, either." Laurel could also add her father to the list of people who might want her dead. She had no plans to trust any of them.

"Somehow, he'll get to you," Dorothy added. "Jericho, too. Theo wants him dead because of what you two did to him. He blames both of you for ruining his life. Just be careful."

"Is Theo the one shooting at the sheriff's office right now?" Laurel asked.

But Dorothy didn't answer her. "No!" the woman shouted, and it was followed by an ear-piercing scream.

And a gunshot.

This one hadn't come from immediately outside the building, either. It had come from the other end of the phone.

"Dorothy?" Laurel said. "What happened?"

Nothing. The line was dead.

Maybe Dorothy was, too. Did that mean Theo had had his own mother shot? Or was this some kind of trick?

Laurel debated whether she should tell Jericho about the call, but it would have to wait. The bullets were still slamming into the front of the building, and she didn't want to say or do anything to distract him. Hopefully soon, the Rangers or backup would arrive and help put a stop to this.

Whatever *this* was.

Two attacks of sheriff offices in the same night. Yes, the one in Sweetwater Springs was no doubt to get the fake evidence that Jericho had leaked. But then why had it stopped? And why were the gunmen now attacking them here? They must know there were lawmen inside. Four of them. Hardly a fortress, but the gunmen, and their boss, had to be desperate to try to shoot their way inside.

"Hell," she heard Jericho say, and again she nearly bolted out from beneath the desk to make sure he hadn't been hurt. By now, some of those bullets had to be getting through.

But Laurel didn't get the chance to bolt.

Everything happened fast. There was a crashing sound behind her, followed by the howl of the security alarm. Before she could even turn around, the glass from the window came flying out over the room. If it was bullet resistant, then something big had shattered it.

Then a hulking-size man wearing dark-colored camouflage scrambled through the gaping hole and grabbed her. She fought him. Tried to scream out for help. But she didn't manage even that before another man on the other side of the window took hold of her and pulled her through.

"Laurel!" Jericho shouted. And even over the sounds of the continuing shots and the alarm, she heard him running toward the office.

But it was too late.

She landed on the ground outside the window. So did both of her attackers. One turned and fired shots into the office window.

Right where Jericho would be.

Oh, God.

Had the man managed to shoot him?

Laurel couldn't see. Couldn't hear much of anything now with the roar of her heartbeat in her ears and the shots that were no longer buffered by the wall. They were loud, thick blasts.

Too many of them.

One of the men stuffed a gag in her mouth, and they continued to drag her away from the window. Away from Jericho.

There was white smoke snaking through the air. From the explosion, no doubt, but part of it also seemed to be freezing fog. The men ran right into it, using it to conceal them.

Using it to kidnap her.

She stumbled, on purpose, and when the thug on the right reached for her, she brought up her foot and kicked him. He growled in pain, latched on to her hair and kept moving.

When the smoke cleared, Laurel saw where they were taking her. To a black car parked beside a Dumpster. If they got her inside, they'd be able to speed away, so she knew she had to keep fighting. Because this wasn't just a kidnapping. Laurel had no doubts that she'd soon be dead if she didn't do something right away.

She twisted her body. Tried to fall again. But the man still had hold of her hair, and he used that to control her. The pain watered her eyes. The fear had her by the throat. But she kept fighting. Kept trying to get away.

"Laurel?" Jericho shouted again.

He was alive. For now. But the gunman turned again and fired a shot in the direction of Jericho's voice.

She prayed he hadn't been hit. Prayed that Jericho would get to her in time.

But he didn't.

The moment the men reached the car, the door flew open. And the men began to drag Laurel inside.

Chapter Seventeen

Jericho couldn't believe what was happening. One second Laurel had been in his office. Now she wasn't.

He had to get to her. Had to stop whatever was happening to her because he knew whatever it was—it would only get worse.

"What happened?" Reese Jenkins, the reserve deputy, came rushing to the doorway.

"They got Laurel."

Jericho scrambled through what was left of the window. And immediately had to duck right back down to dodge the bullet that blasted through the air. However, he did get a glimpse of Laurel.

And the two armed thugs that were on either side of her. He also got a glimpse of the car that'd been hidden by the Dumpster. Since it was out of line of sight of any part of the sheriff's building, Jericho had no idea how long it'd been there, but there was a road just behind it. The men were heading in that direction, and heading fast, so it was clear that's how they planned to escape with Laurel.

Jericho called out to her. Only to have another bullet come his way.

Still, he could see that she was fighting to get free. Could also see that one of the men had her in a fierce grip—literally dragging her by her hair and trying to put her in the car.

"Cover me," Jericho shouted to Reese. "And don't you dare hit Laurel with friendly fire."

He doubted that it was possible for Reese to actually cover him since the gunmen at the front of the building were still shooting. But Jericho couldn't just stay put. He had to try to get to Laurel and stop those hired guns.

Reese gave a shaky nod and hurried to the side of the window. He leaned out, took aim while Jericho climbed through and dropped to the ground. The bitter cold hit him right off. So did the smoke lingering from the explosion. Jericho ignored both and started running.

He didn't get far.

The thug on Laurel's left turned, fired. Jericho had to drop down behind a cruiser. It wasn't just one shot, either. At least six bullets came his way, pinning him down.

Reese didn't fire. Probably because he didn't have a clean shot. But Jericho heard a sound he damn sure didn't want to hear.

The roar of the car's engine.

He peered around the cruiser and his heart missed a couple of beats. Because the driver hit the accelerator. They were getting away.

Cursing, Jericho fished through his pocket, found the master key for the cruiser and managed to get the door open. Not easily. Because the gunmen out front started shooting at him. He practically jumped inside once he had it open, and the moment he had the engine started, he hit the accelerator, heading after the black car.

The road behind the sheriff's office was narrow, coiling through a neighborhood with walls of houses on each side. Plenty of trees, too. Lots of places for hired guns to wait so they could attack. He only hoped that bullets didn't start flying here or plenty of innocent people could be hurt.

Finally, they reached the edge of the neighborhood, and the black car took a turn into the town's park. Onto an even more narrow road. Sometime during the past hour or so, a light mist had started to fall, and it had created some ice scabs on the road. Jericho hit one, went into a skid but fought to regain control of the cruiser.

Ahead of him, the driver of the black car wasn't so lucky.

Jericho could only watch as the car veered

hard to the right. The wheels clipped the sidewalk, ricocheting the vehicle to the left.

And it slammed into a streetlight.

Oh, man. It was as if a Roman candle went off in his head. Laurel could have been hurt or worse. The front end of the car was a tangled mess, and there was steam spewing out of what was left of the engine.

Jericho brought the cruiser to a quick stop just a few feet behind the wrecked car, and he hurried out, leaving the door open in case he had to grab Laurel and jump right back in. That's when he spotted the swirling blue lights from a cruiser coming up the road behind him. Reese, no doubt. Maybe even Levi.

Good. Because Jericho would probably need plenty of backup.

Maybe an ambulance, too.

With his gun ready, Jericho approached the car. However, before he got there, the back door opened and someone got out. Not easily. The person was groaning as if in pain.

Laurel.

She looked up, and when she spotted him, she started to run toward him. Jericho ran, too, and quickly ate up the distance between them. She was alive, but there was blood on her head. Maybe other injuries that he couldn't see.

Nor could Jericho take the time to find out.

Because a second person came out of the car. It was the same thug that'd dragged Laurel by the hair. The guy was still armed, and even though he staggered a little, he still managed to point the gun at Laurel.

He fired.

Jericho hooked his arm around Laurel's waist and yanked her behind the door of his cruiser. Not a moment too soon, because another shot came right at them. Apparently, the gunman hadn't been injured in the wreck. And neither had his shooting buddy, Jericho quickly learned, when the second gunman got out, too. He didn't waste any time joining in on the shooting fest.

This was exactly what Jericho had hoped to avoid. Here, Laurel was under attack again, and all those stray bullets could be going into the nearby neighborhood.

"Get in," Jericho told her.

She was still wobbly, so Jericho gave her a shove. He also sent a couple of rounds in the direction of the gunmen, but was careful to keep the shots low, so if they missed the men completely, they'd go into the ground.

Behind him, the other cruiser braked to a stop. Levi stepped out, using his own door for cover. A good thing, too, because the idiots started sending some of their shots his way.

"We need to get out of here," Jericho called

out to his brother. Levi darn sure didn't argue with that.

Laurel crawled to the passenger's seat so that Jericho could get behind the wheel. He threw the car into gear, ready to hit the gas, but an SUV came flying out from a side road to their right. Jericho couldn't see who was inside. But it didn't take him long to figure out what they wanted.

Whoever was inside the SUV opened fire.

THEY WERE CAUGHT in a crossfire.

The blood rushed to Laurel's head, and the punch of fear robbed her of what little breath she had left. She was thankful to be out of the car with the men who'd taken her, but now Jericho was right back in the middle of a deadly situation.

His brother and the deputy, too.

And there was nothing she could do but stay down and pray that they would all get out of this alive.

The gunmen in the SUV didn't waste any time shooting at the tires of the cruiser, and Laurel felt the exact moment they managed to do just that. Jericho still threw the cruiser into gear, no doubt ready to try to get them out of there.

But then Laurel heard the plinging sound.

Someone in the SUV had tossed something onto the road just in front of them.

"Get down!" Jericho shouted. "It's a grenade." He threw himself over her, pushing her down on the seat.

Just as the blast tore through the air.

The impact was so hard that it lifted the front of the cruiser and sent it flying back several feet before they crashed to the ground. Because of the way Jericho and she were hunkered down, their heads hit the dashboard, hard. Hard enough for her to see stars.

Laurel immediately looked back to check on Jericho and gasped when she saw the blood trickling down his forehead.

"It's just a cut," he explained. "Same with you."

She touched her fingers to her own forehead, felt the warm blood, but she was too shaken to feel the pain. Too shaken to move.

But Jericho didn't seem to have that problem.

He'd managed to keep hold of his gun, and he took another one from the glove compartment. "Stay down," he insisted.

However, he didn't do that. He sat up, his gaze darting around and pausing for a moment on the rearview mirror.

"Levi and the deputy," she said, trying to get up. "Are they okay?"

"They appear to be." Jericho pushed her back on the seat and tried to start the cruiser engine.

Nothing.

It'd obviously been damaged too much in the explosion. No doubt what their attackers had planned. Now they were sitting ducks in the crossfire. But maybe they could somehow get to Levi's vehicle. Or better yet, maybe they could take out these gunmen.

"The men in the SUV aren't shooting at us," Jericho mumbled.

Because her ears were still ringing, it took Laurel a moment to understand what he'd said. And to realize it was true. The men in the SUV were shooting at the thugs in the black car. And vice versa. The bullets were no longer coming at Jericho and her.

What the heck was going on?

From the moment she'd seen that SUV come out from the side road, Laurel had assumed they were working with the men in the black car. But clearly they weren't if they were trying to kill each other. However, Laurel doubted that meant whoever survived would just let them walk away.

"Will backup come?" she asked.

"Eventually. I figure Levi probably called the second reserve deputy, Shane. He might respond alone, but Shane's a rookie. No experience with chasing down bad guys. He'll probably wait for the Rangers to arrive so he can bring them here."

"Where are the Rangers?" was her next question.

"Too far away. It'll be a good half hour."

She groaned. So they were on their own, because she doubted this attack would last that long.

Laurel tried to steady her nerves. Hard to do with the danger right on top of them. Added to that, she was past the stage of just shivering. When the men had dragged her through the office window, she hadn't been wearing a coat, and now that the engine was disabled, it was getting cold fast in the interior of the cruiser.

Jericho's phone buzzed, and he passed it to her to answer. That's when she saw Levi's name on the screen.

"Were you hurt?" Levi asked before she could say anything.

"Just minor stuff." Laurel wiped the blood from her head, reached up and did the same to Jericho. "How about the two of you?"

"We're both fine. But we got an even bigger problem than the SUV and the black car. Another vehicle just pulled up behind us. A limo. The headlights are off, but when one of the people inside opened the door, I got a glimpse of a two guys in the front seat with guns. I'm betting we've got more gunmen joining this sick shooting party. I'll call you back if I can figure out what the heck is going on."

God, no. Not more of them. Whoever was behind this had hired an army to kill them.

Laurel was about to relay the info to Jericho, but his attention was on the rearview mirror again. "I see the limo." And he added some more profanity.

"Are they shooting, too?" Laurel asked. There were so many bullets being fired that it was hard to tell.

"Not yet." But Jericho no longer had his attention on the newcomers. He was watching the exchange of gunfire between the others. "Two down," he said. "Lots more to go."

And then the gunfire stopped.

Laurel lifted her head just enough to see that the two men in the black car were down. Literally. They were both sprawled out on the ground and likely dead.

But why?

The men in the SUV certainly weren't shooting at whoever was in the limo. Did that mean they were working together?

Before she could even try to come up with what'd just happened, Jericho's phone buzzed again. She answered it without looking at the screen because Laurel figured the call was from Levi.

It wasn't.

"Sheriff Crockett," the man said. Laurel didn't recognize his voice. She put the call on speaker so that Jericho could hear it. "Are you listening, Sheriff?"

She connected gazes with Jericho, silently asking if she knew the caller, but he shook his head.

"Who are you and what do you want?" Jericho snarled.

"I'm in the limo behind your brother. Let's just say I'm a friend trying to do you a favor. We don't want you. Only Laurel. Hand her over, and you, your kin and the deputy can leave."

Laurel hadn't thought her heart could beat any faster, but she was wrong. This attack was all for her. And it didn't matter exactly that she didn't know who was doing it or why it was happening, she'd put Jericho and heaven knew who else in danger.

"That's not going to happen," Jericho answered, still keeping watch around them. "Now, who the hell are you?"

"My name's not important."

"Yeah, it is. Because I want to know who to

arrest or kill. Your choice. Either way is fine with me, but you're not getting Laurel."

"Then you'll have to pay a big price for that decision. There are roadblocks in every direction. Explosives. Anyone who tries to get to you now will pay. Is that what you want?"

"Text Levi," Jericho mouthed to her. "Let him know."

Even though her hands were shaking, Laurel managed to do what Jericho asked without hanging up on the snake who was making these threats.

"Why do you want me?" she asked the man once she was finished sending the text.

Jericho shot her a nasty look, probably because he hadn't wanted her to have any verbal contact with the goon, but Laurel wasn't going to stay quiet.

"It's nothing personal," the man answered. "Just doing my job."

Well, it was very personal to her. People she cared about were in danger. "And who paid you to do that job?" she pressed.

The man didn't answer, and even though she couldn't be sure, it seemed as if he was having a whispered conversation with someone. Probably someone in the limo with him.

Laurel pushed the phone against her chest so the caller wouldn't be able to hear what she was about to say, and she looked up at Jericho. "I don't want you to die, but this might—"

"No way," he interrupted. "I'm not handing you over to them."

It was exactly what Laurel had expected him to say. But she had to make him at least consider it. "I don't want to die, but if those men manage to kill both of us, then Maddox will be an orphan. I don't want that, either."

"You really think our *friend* will let us all live? Not a chance. Because if he lets me walk, I'll hunt him down. And I'll kill him."

Yes, Jericho would. And the man on the other end of the line almost certainly knew that, too.

"Enough of this." Jericho snatched the phone from her hand. "Who the hell hired you to come after Laurel?"

More silence. It went on so long that Laurel thought the line might have gone dead. But it hadn't.

"I hired him," someone finally answered.

And this time, it was a voice that Laurel had no trouble recognizing.

Chapter Eighteen

Dorothy.

Jericho wasn't sure which of their suspects would turn out to be behind this, but none of them would have been a surprise. All had motive.

Or at least they thought they had motive.

"You're doing this because of the money you lost on those business deals?" Jericho snapped.

"In part," Dorothy admitted. "But I really don't want to discuss that now. Is everything in place?" she asked, and it took Jericho a moment to realize that she wasn't talking to him.

"It's in place," a man verified. The same man who'd been talking to them earlier. One of Dorothy's hired thugs.

Jericho was about to demand to know what exactly was *in place*, but then he heard Reese's shout. "I'm sorry, Jericho. I didn't see them in time."

Heck. That couldn't be good. Jericho turned

around, trying to pick through the darkness, and he finally saw what he didn't want to see.

Levi and Reese.

Their hands were in the air, and there was a gunman on each side of the cruiser his brother had been driving.

"Don't blame the deputy or your brother." Dorothy's voice had gone from sarcastic to taunting. "I brought plenty of backup with me, and there were men waiting in the ditch."

And it'd worked. It also meant Dorothy had at least six gunmen with her. Two in the SUV, the two guarding Levi and Reese, and the two that Levi had spotted in the limo when it first arrived.

Of course, there could be more.

Not to mention Dorothy was probably armed. He hoped she was because he couldn't shoot an unarmed woman, but he darn sure could shoot an armed one. Especially this one.

"Is Theo helping you?" Jericho came right out and asked.

"Please. I have a coward of a son. He hired those men in the black car to save you, to kidnap you."

Laurel shook her head. "Why?

"Because Theo was going to keep you all for himself so he could try to convince you that he's the man for you. Laughable, isn't it?"

"Not really," Jericho growled. "Nothing laughable about this. So, you lost money. Boo-hoo—"

"I lost more than that!" Dorothy paused, and Jericho figured she was trying to get hold of the temper tantrum she'd just started. "I lost my reputation. My so-called friends whisper behind my back now. And that's all because of Laurel."

"How do you figure that?" Jericho asked.

"She was supposed to marry Theo. I told everyone it was finally going to happen. I made plans for business deals that hinged on Theo and Laurel being man and wife."

All right. Jericho didn't want to have this conversation, but it might give him time to figure out what to do next. "You mean plans with Rossman and Cawley? Who, by the way, are both dead. Your doing?"

She didn't confirm the part about having them murdered. "Bigger plans than that. Ones that would have made me richer than my wildest dreams."

"Ah, I get it now. You made those plans because of Laurel and her father's connections. When the engagement ended, so did the connections, and you were left holding a very empty bag that you hoped would be filled with money."

Again, Dorothy didn't verbally confirm it, but judging from her ripe profanity, he'd hit pay dirt.

"Laurel ruined us," Dorothy said a moment later. "Both Theo and me."

"I didn't ruin you," Laurel argued. "You did it to yourself."

"You did this!" she shouted. "And after all that, Theo still wants you back. Even after I told him that you had crawled into bed with that cowboy."

Even though Laurel was scared spitless, that put some fire in her eyes. "Jericho's my husband."

"Right," Dorothy said with a serious dose of sarcasm. "A marriage of necessity to stop your father from getting custody of your son. Well, I don't think you have to worry about that anymore."

Jericho wondered if that meant that Dorothy had killed Herschel. No such luck. Because a moment later, Herschel got out of the limo. Not voluntarily. A heavily muscled armed goon shoved him out.

Herschel staggered, and it took him several wobbly steps to regain his balance. The man's hands were cuffed in front of him, and he looked disheveled. Definitely not a happy camper right now.

"Give me Laurel or Herschel dies," Dorothy threatened.

Jericho so wished the woman could see the

flat look he was giving her. "Do you think I really care a flying fig what you do to Herschel?"

Laurel made a sound of agreement. After everything Herschel had tried to do to her, Jericho thought she might be willing to pull the trigger herself. She certainly wasn't going to sacrifice herself for him.

And that sent an uneasy feeling snaking up his spine.

If Dorothy thought she could use Herschel to lure out Laurel, then the woman had something up her sleeve.

Something dirty, no doubt.

"Oh, you should care about what happens to Herschel," Dorothy said. She was back to being as cold as ice. No sign of that hot temper right now. "If you want to know the truth, that is."

"What truth?" Laurel and Jericho asked at the same time.

Herschel certainly didn't jump to answer. Thanks to the interior lights from the limo, Jericho had no trouble seeing the man's expression. Not defeat. He was riled to the core.

"The truth about your father's death," Dorothy finally said. She stepped from the limo wearing a thick fur coat. And she was smiling. "Or should I say, his murder? Because Sherman Crockett was indeed murdered."

That uneasy feeling inside him turned to a

full roar. "What do you know about that?" Jericho demanded.

"Plenty. I know Herschel murdered him, and I have proof. Not with me, of course. I'm not stupid. But I have it tucked safely away."

Jericho figured this was about the time for Herschel to blurt out his innocence. He didn't. Nor did he deny that Dorothy had such proof.

"Let's just say Herschel had too much to drink one night and got very chatty," Dorothy explained. "He didn't know I was recording every word he said."

Now Herschel responded. His narrowed gaze cut to Dorothy, and he cursed her. "You'll burn in hell for this."

"Maybe, but you'll be right there with me." Dorothy patted his cheek before looking toward Jericho again. "Hand over Laurel, and I'll give you Herschel and the proof."

So, that's what was up her sleeve. Laurel for the thing that Dorothy thought Jericho wanted the most.

"You can be the one to arrest Herschel. And you can be there when he gets the needle shoved into his arm," Dorothy continued. "Think about it, Jericho."

He didn't have to think about it. Yes, he wanted justice. He wanted it so much that he could taste it.

But there was no way he'd trade Laurel for it.

"No deal," Jericho let the woman know.

"Too bad." Dorothy answered quickly enough that she'd no doubt considered that's how this would play out.

"Why do you want Laurel alive, anyway?" Jericho asked.

"Because she'll force me to go through with those business deals," Laurel provided. "She needs my contacts, and my signature. And once she has that, she'll kill me."

Jericho had no doubts, none, that it was exactly what Dorothy had in mind. Either way, she'd kill Laurel first chance she got.

"I suggest you change your mind," Dorothy warned him. "Because if you don't hand Laurel over to me, I'll give my men the order to start shooting. You're outnumbered, Jericho. Outgunned, too. They'll kill all of you, including Laurel."

Jericho knew this wasn't a bluff. If Dorothy couldn't have Laurel, then she'd have them all killed. Or try.

That was a risk. One that cut him to the core. But at least Laurel was inside the cruiser, and even though the engine was damaged, the windows and the sides were bullet resistant. His brother and Reese were also still close enough to their cruiser that they could use it for cover when all hell broke loose.

He hoped.

"Stay down," Jericho whispered to Laurel. He took another gun from the glove compartment and also handed her extra magazines of ammo. "No matter what happens, don't get out."

Laurel's eyes widened, and she shook her head. "What are you going to do?"

"Stay down," he repeated, and brushed a kiss on her mouth.

"Levi, you ready to do something about this?" Jericho shouted.

"Oh, yeah," his brother confirmed without hesitation.

Just as Jericho had thought. That was the only green light he needed.

Jericho came out of the cruiser with guns blazing.

"NO!" LAUREL SHOUTED to Jericho. But it was already too late. He was out of the cruiser, and the shots started flying.

Sweet heaven, he was going to get killed.

Maybe Levi and the deputy would be, too. Of course, it wasn't as if Dorothy had given them too many options. And now Laurel could only pray that they got out of this alive.

Dorothy screamed out her own "No!" and

Laurel wondered if she'd been shot. Maybe. But she quickly had to amend that when the woman belted out another order. "Kill them all. Do it now."

Laurel lifted her head just enough to see out the back window. No sign of Dorothy. The woman had probably gotten back in the limo. Laurel's father was on the ground, his hands covering his head. Trying to protect himself.

Dorothy's gunmen were doing the same thing—they'd gotten behind the back of the limo. Out of the line of fire but still in a position to shoot and carry out Dorothy's orders. It was the same for Levi and Reese. They were on the side of their cruiser, both of them shooting.

Jericho ducked down behind the door of the cruiser, once again using it for cover, but he continued to lift his head enough to return fire. So many shots came at him. Too many, and Laurel sat there, feeling helpless. And furious that Dorothy wanted her dead all because of money and revenge.

She thought of her son, and it broke her heart to think that she might not see him again. But at least he wasn't here in the middle of the attack.

From the corner of her eye, Laurel saw the movement. The two gunmen from the SUV were getting into position to help out their fellow hired thugs. One of them scrambled toward the hole in the pavement created by the grenade.

Coming toward Jericho and her.

And not just coming toward them. The guy was trying to sneak up on Jericho so he could gun him down from behind.

Laurel didn't think. She just reacted. She opened the cruiser door just enough so that she could take aim and stop him. But he must have seen what she was doing because he pivoted in her direction, bringing up his gun to shoot her.

But Laurel shot first.

The recoil of the gun stunned her a moment, but she quickly fired another shot. Both of the bullets slammed into the man's chest. However, he didn't drop to the ground. He stood there, frozen, his gun still pointed at her for what seemed an eternity.

Before he finally collapsed.

Jericho snapped toward her, and Laurel braced herself for his usual protest—*what word of* stay down *didn't you hear?*—but he muttered, "Thanks," followed by "Now, get down and stay there."

The words had barely left his mouth when he levered himself up, turned and fired in the direction of the SUV. But not at the SUV itself. At the second gunman. Laurel had been so focused on

Jericho and the man she'd killed that she hadn't noticed the second one.

But he'd seen her.

He had his gun aimed right at her and was no doubt within a split second of pulling the trigger.

Jericho beat him to it.

He finished off the gunman with a shot to the head, and in the same motion, Jericho turned his gun toward the limo. He fired. And he took out the gunman on the left-rear side.

Laurel hated to feel relief that she'd just killed a man and had watched another die, but the relief came, anyway. They were winning. Except she knew that could change on a dime.

"Don't shoot!" someone yelled. It was the final remaining gunman. "I'm surrendering."

Laurel wasn't sure if it was some kind of trick, but then she saw the man slowly get up from the limo's right side. He still had hold of his gun, but he raised his hands in the air.

"Drop your weapon," Jericho ordered. He stayed behind the cover of the door. Good. Because this still wasn't over. "Are there any other gunmen in the limo?"

He tossed down his gun, shook his head. "Just the boss lady. Don't shoot me. Arrange for me to get a plea deal, and I'll tell you whatever you want to know."

"Where's the proof that Herschel killed my father," Jericho demanded.

The gunman shook his head. "I don't know that, but I know plenty about the men she hired to kill you. That's something you'll want, right? It'll be enough to put her in jail for the rest of her life."

Before Jericho could answer, Laurel heard the sound. It didn't even sound human at first, more like something that would come from a feral animal. But it was Dorothy. And it was the sound of pure outrage.

"Coward!" she screamed.

"Dorothy, get out of the car," Jericho ordered her.

"If you kill me, you'll never get the evidence I have against Herschel. Never," Dorothy threatened.

Laurel figured the woman would use that to bargain while she stayed in the limo. She didn't. Making another of those feral sounds, Dorothy came out from the backseat. A gun in each hand.

And she fired shots at Jericho.

Jericho ducked down in the nick of time, the bullets slamming into the cruiser door.

The woman didn't give up. She kept firing. Kept screaming. Until Levi took aim at her and brought her down with a shot to the chest.

Dorothy fell, the guns clattering to the frozen ground with her.

"I'm sorry," Levi immediately said to Jericho. "I wanted to take her alive."

Laurel understood that. She also understood it'd been impossible to do that. It was clear Dorothy would have murdered them all if she'd gotten the chance.

"Don't get out," Jericho insisted when Laurel pushed open the door. He glanced around, no doubt looking for more of Dorothy's hired thugs. Laurel didn't close the door, but she did duck back inside.

"There aren't any more of us, I swear," the lone surviving gunman insisted, and he repeated his earlier offer. "I'll tell you what you want to know."

But Jericho didn't turn his attention toward the gunman. He went to Dorothy. Leaned down and checked her pulse. He didn't have to confirm that the woman was indeed dead because Laurel could tell from his expression that she was.

Levi hurried to the gunman, kicking his gun aside and cuffing him. Reese headed out to check on the other gunmen. No doubt to make sure they were dead, as well.

However, Jericho went to her father. Jericho caught onto the collar of Herschel's coat and dragged him to his feet. "Where's the proof that you murdered my father?"

It wasn't exactly a request. Jericho moved until he was right in Herschel's face.

But Herschel just laughed.

She saw Jericho struggling to hold on to his temper. Laurel didn't blame him. He'd loved his father, and now Sherman's killer was right there in front of him.

Despite Jericho's order for her to stay put, Laurel got out. She was already chilled to the bone, and the gust of bitter wind didn't help. Nor did the fact that it'd started to snow.

Laurel hurried toward the others and hoped there was a shred of fatherly love left in Herschel. Enough of a thread for him to come clean.

"Where's the evidence Dorothy had?" Laurel asked him, moving next to Jericho.

Her father's gaze went from Jericho to her. Then to the wedding ring she was wearing. He smiled. Not an ordinary one. Definitely not one filled with any fatherly love whatsoever. Laurel had always figured he hated her, but that smile and the look in his eyes was all the proof she needed.

Jericho looked ready to unleash his temper and his fists on Herschel, but then his gaze met hers. She could almost see the battle going on inside him. Could feel it. That's why she was surprised when Jericho took a step back.

"Levi, I need some cuffs." Jericho's voice wasn't exactly calm, his muscles weren't anywhere near relaxed, but he sounded exactly like the lawman that he was. "Herschel, you're under arrest for Quinn Rossman's murder." And Jericho continued to read him his rights.

"I didn't kill him," her father insisted. "And I can prove I was lured to the crime scene so his death could be pinned on me. Hell, I'm betting Dorothy's hired idiot will tell you the same thing."

Judging from the gunman's stark expression, he would do just that.

Levi handed Jericho the cuffs, and he slapped them on her father.

But Herschel only laughed when Levi took him toward the cruiser. "With the lawyers on my payroll, I'll be out of jail in no time," her father insisted. "This isn't over."

And, yes, it sounded exactly like the threat that it was.

Chapter Nineteen

Jericho cursed the whole white-Christmas thing. It was snowing, and yeah, it was pretty all right. It'd make for a picture-perfect holiday, but with the ice already on the road, it was slowing down the drive to the safe house.

Laurel was next to him in the front of the cruiser; Levi, in the back. His brother was on the phone, but Laurel leaned forward and stared up at the night sky as if cursing it, too. It was a toss-up as to who was the most antsy about getting to the safe house so they could see Maddox. They knew the baby was fine, thanks to several conversations with Jax, but Jericho wouldn't rest easy until he saw his son. Of course, resting easy was a pipe dream, anyway.

No doubt for Laurel, as well.

They both had nicks on their faces. Both looked as if they'd been through the wringer and back. That's why it surprised him when she looked at him and smiled.

"It's still a couple of hours until Christmas," she said. "We didn't miss spending it with him. Well, we won't if the weather doesn't slow us down too much."

"We'll be there soon."

They were only a few miles away, but Jericho needed to drive around a little longer. The only thing good about going at a snail's pace was that he could make sure Laurel and he weren't being followed.

Not that the chances were high they would be.

Jericho hadn't started the drive to the safe house until the Rangers were fairly sure they'd rounded up all of Herschel's hired thugs. While the Rangers had been doing that, Jericho had arrested Herschel, and Theo and Dorothy's gunman who'd surrendered at the scene. All three were behind bars.

"I killed a man," Laurel said. It wasn't exactly out of the blue. Jericho figured it'd been weighing on her mind along with everything else.

"You killed a *bad* man," he clarified. "One who would have murdered all of us if he'd gotten the chance. You stopped him."

She made a sound of agreement followed by a sigh. Of course, she knew that already, but it would give her nightmares for a while. Him, too. Jericho had gotten a few years shaved off his life when he'd seen her open the cruiser door, putting herself in the line of fire. For him.

"You saved my life," he added. "Thanks for that."

Laurel brushed a kiss on his cheek. "And you saved mine. But I need to thank you more than once since I lost count of how many times you saved me."

He looked at her, barely a glance because he had to keep his eyes on the road. However, he wished he could just hold her.

All right, kiss her, too.

Just being with Laurel would make him feel a whole lot better.

"Keep pressing him," Levi insisted to the person on the other end of his phone. He finished his latest call with one of the Rangers, but judging from the way he shoved his phone back in his pocket, he wasn't happy with the outcome of the conversation.

"A problem?" But Jericho hated to even ask. Hated more to hear the answer because it was probably one he didn't want to hear. "Are Herschel and Theo still behind bars?"

"They're still there. For now. Theo's been officially charged with kidnapping Laurel from the sheriff's office."

"Good," she said, but there wasn't much joy in her tone, and when she settled her head against his shoulder again—something she'd been doing on and off since the drive started—Jericho noticed she was still trembling.

"Dorothy's gunman is cooperating," Levi went on. "That's the good news. The bad news is that he confessed to assisting in both Cawley's and Rossman's murders."

Hell in a handbasket.

That didn't help Laurel's trembling. Because she knew what it meant. With that confession, Herschel wouldn't be charged with those murders.

"Is my father getting out of jail?" she asked.

"Not tonight. The Rangers can hold him for questioning while they go through the evidence we got from Theo. There should be enough in that to make some charges stick for his attempt to have Laurel declared mentally incompetent."

Yeah, but those weren't charges for murder. Not for Rossman's, anyway. And not for Jericho's father. Levi's and Laurel's silence let him know that they were thinking the same thing.

"I'm sorry," Laurel finally said. She paused. "Can you get the DA to offer Theo a deal? If he knows where his mother put the recording of my father's drunk confession, then could he exchange that for a lesser sentence?"

"No. I want Theo behind bars for a long time for what he did to you."

"So do I. But more than that, I want justice for your father. Think it through," she added when Jericho opened his mouth to argue. "If my father's out of jail, we'll never be free to live our lives with Maddox."

Well, he certainly couldn't argue with that. "We can get Herschel some other way."

"Not as fast as you can by having the DA strike a deal with Theo. Theo's facing several felony charges, and he'll get years of jail time. My father could get life in prison. Maybe even the death penalty."

"Laurel's right," Levi piped in.

She was. But it felt as if he was minimizing what'd happened to her. Still, Herschel would do far worse than kidnapping if he got the chance. Now that Laurel had rejected him, Herschel would be even more intent on seeing them all dead.

"Make the call," Jericho told his brother. "See if Theo's willing to deal, and if he is, contact the DA and work it out."

That caused Laurel to settle even closer to him. He probably should have told her to tighten her seat belt, but Jericho wanted this contact as much as she seemed to want it.

"You said 'free to live our lives with Maddox.' Did you mean it?" Jericho asked.

Laurel lifted her head. Blinked. "Of course." Then her eyes widened. "Oh, I guess that sounded bold. I need to give you a free pass."

"Excuse me? What the heck does that mean?"

She glanced back at Levi, maybe to make sure his brother was on the phone and not listening to them. He was. Well, he was on the phone, anyway.

"A free pass for the sex," she said. "Just so you know, I don't expect anything because we slept together. And I don't expect anything because of this." She lifted her hand, tapped the wedding ring.

"Well, you should." He said that a whole lot louder than he'd intended. And yes, it got Levi's attention, but Jericho didn't care. This conversation couldn't wait. "You should expect everything from me."

"Everything?" Laurel asked, sounding very uncertain of what that meant.

Jericho wasn't exactly certain, either. Not of the details, anyway, but he had a bead on the big picture. "I'm your husband, and I'd like to keep it that way."

He shot his brother a glare in the rearview mirror when Levi smiled. Maybe the smile meant that Levi approved of this marriage, or maybe it was just that whole thing of him watching his big brother squirm.

"You'd like to keep it that way?" Laurel repeated, still sounding uncertain.

Jericho would have attempted to clarify that, but that's when Levi's smile vanished, and he slid his hand over his phone.

"Theo didn't ask for us to work out a plea deal with the DA for him to get a lighter sentence. He told the Rangers where they could find the evidence against Herschel," Levi interrupted. "It's at Dorothy's house in San Antonio. The local cops are headed over there now."

That was great news, but that wasn't a great-news kind of look on Levi's face. "What's wrong?" Jericho asked.

"Theo's on the line, and he wants to talk to Laurel."

Jericho wanted to growl out a "no way in hell," but it wasn't his call, and Laurel reached for the phone before he could say anything.

She jabbed the speaker button. "Thank you for doing the right thing about the evidence," Laurel greeted Theo. "I appreciate it. So do the Crocketts. But I'm not getting back together with you."

"I know," Theo readily admitted.

"But yet you'll give us the evidence. Why?" she demanded.

A good question. Jericho hoped Theo had a good answer.

"Let's call it a wedding gift. With no strings attached," Theo said. "I know you don't believe me, but I sent those men to save you tonight. I knew my mother was going to try to kill you, and I thought if I could hide you away, she wouldn't be able to get to you."

"Laurel was already safe," Jericho snarled. "You could have gotten her killed."

"I know that now. And I'm sorry."

Theo sounded sincere enough, but Jericho would make sure he got the maximum sentence.

"I don't want you in my life," Laurel said to Theo.

"I won't be. Good luck, Laurel. I sincerely hope you're happy, even if that happiness happens to be with Jericho."

Laurel didn't respond. She just handed the phone back to Levi. "You believe him?" she asked.

Jericho was surprised that he did. "With all the charges against him, Theo's looking at a decade or two in jail. He could have withheld the evidence as part of a plea deal with the DA. He didn't."

That didn't mean Jericho wouldn't be checking to make sure Theo did all the jail time and then stayed far away from Laurel.

She nodded. "Good. Then, we can get Maddox and move on with our lives."

There it was again. Not yours or mine. *Our lives.*

Jericho liked the sound of that. Figured he would like the sound of it even more when they saw their son. He took the final turn toward the safe house.

The snow was coming down harder here, and the house was already dusted with it. His son would wake up to a white Christmas. No gifts, though. But Jericho would remedy that. Unless the snow piled up, they'd be able to leave in the morning, and he could call the owner of the department store and beg him to open so that Jericho could do a quick shopping trip.

The moment he pulled the cruiser to a stop, the door opened, and his brother Jax came out. As expected, Jax had his bag ready and looked more than ready to leave. And no doubt was. He wanted to get home so he could spend Christmas with his own son.

"Glad you're in one piece," Jax greeted them, and then he glanced at the cuts on Laurel's and his head. "Well, for the most part."

"Thanks for everything," Jericho told him. He used his sleeve to wipe the blood from Laurel's and his face. Best for his mom and Maddox not to see that. "You should get going before the roads get bad."

Jax nodded, started toward his car but then stopped. "Are you two back together?" But he waved off the question. Smiled. "Of course you are. Heck, you were never really apart. Merry Christmas."

It was Jericho's go-to reaction to scowl at a remark like that, but he had to admit to himself that it was true. Laurel and he were back together.

He hoped.

Now he needed to see how Laurel felt about that.

However, Jericho didn't get the chance to say anything because the door opened again, and his mother gathered the three of them inside. There was a fire snapping and flickering in the stone fireplace, and the deputies were at the small kitchen table drinking what smelled like hot chocolate.

"Where's Maddox?" Laurel and Jericho asked in unison.

His mother put her finger to her lips and motioned for them to follow her to one of the bedrooms. Levi didn't follow them. His phone buzzed, and he stayed in the living room to answer it.

There wasn't a crib in the safe house, but they

found Maddox sleeping on the center of the bed with pillows around the edges so that he wouldn't fall off.

Laurel got to him first, and she pressed a flurry of kisses on Maddox's face. Jericho soon got his turn, and even though he wanted his son to get plenty of sleep, he wasn't disappointed when Maddox opened his eyes. The little boy gave a sleepy yawn, but then he smiled the moment his gaze landed on them.

"Da-Da," Maddox babbled, his smile aimed at Jericho.

Jericho nearly lost it.

"I've been showing him your picture and telling him you're his daddy," Iris explained. "I hope you don't mind," she said to Laurel.

"No, I don't mind at all."

Hearing that one word was one of the best Christmas presents he'd ever gotten.

And then he got another one.

"Wuv you," Maddox said, and he repeated it to Laurel as his eyelids drifted back down.

Jericho couldn't help himself. He had to kiss his boy again. Laurel did, too. And then they eased out of the room and into the hall. They didn't close the door, though. They just stood there and watched Maddox sleep.

"Fatherhood looks good on you, son." Iris gave

him a pat on the arm and then did the same to Laurel before she strolled away.

Jericho had so many things to say to Laurel, but the moment he opened his mouth, Levi started toward them. Jericho groaned at the interruption until he remembered they had important business still up in the air.

"SAPD found the evidence at Dorothy's house," Levi explained. "It was exactly where Theo said it would be. And yes, in the recording, Herschel does confess to having Dad murdered."

Jericho's breath rushed out. Pure relief. Laurel's reaction was pretty much the same. It'd been a long wait for justice, but it'd finally come.

"My father will be charged with murder," she verified. "He'll stay in jail."

"For a very long time," Jericho assured her. There was no bail for murder, so he would stay behind bars while awaiting trial. Considering everything Herschel had done, it was another good Christmas present.

And now Jericho had just one more.

Levi had the sense to go back in the living room and give them some privacy. Well, as much privacy as they could have in a small house filled with people.

"You know what I want for Christmas?" he asked.

Laurel obviously hadn't been expecting that question because she gave him a funny look.

"I want you." Jericho snapped her to him. Kissed her. Not exactly a chaste kiss, either.

She smiled when he finally broke the kiss so they could catch their breath. "I want you, too."

That was a good start, but it wasn't quite enough. So, Jericho kissed her again. He wanted to remind her of what had brought them here.

And it wasn't just the attraction.

It was something much, much more.

He took out the blue rock. The one she'd used when she asked him to marry her. Or rather, when she'd told him that was the way things had to be. Now, he dropped it into the palm of her hand.

"I'm calling in the marker," he said. "I'm in love with you."

Tears watered her eyes, but he was pretty sure they were happy ones. She kissed him. And she was very good at it. Jericho felt himself go warm and then hot in all the right places.

Including his heart.

"Jericho, I've been in love with you most of my life. All of my life," she added.

Now it was his turn to smile. Probably a goofy one, but it was genuine. Laurel loved him.

He brought her closer to him and spelled out

the rest of his wish list. "I want you and Maddox. I want this marriage and our family to be real."

"It already is," she said. Smiling again, Laurel pulled him to her for a long, slow kiss.

* * * * *

Look for more books in USA TODAY
bestselling author Delores Fossen's miniseries
APPALOOSA PASS RANCH
on sale in 2016!

LARGER-PRINT
BOOKS!

◆ HARLEQUIN *Presents*

GET 2 FREE LARGER-PRINT
NOVELS PLUS 2 FREE GIFTS!

PASSION
GUARANTEED
SEDUCTION

LARGER-PRINT BOOKS!

GET 2 FREE LARGER-PRINT NOVELS PLUS
2 FREE GIFTS!

HARLEQUIN®

Romance

From the Heart, For the Heart

YES! Please send me 2 FREE LARGER-PRINT Harlequin® Romance novels and my 2 FREE gifts (gifts are worth about $10). After receiving them, if I don't wish to receive any more books, I can return the shipping statement marked "cancel." If I don't cancel, I will receive 4 brand-new novels every month and be billed just $5.09 per book in the U.S. or $5.49 per book in Canada. That's a savings of at least 15% off the cover price! It's quite a bargain! Shipping and handling is just 50¢ per book in the U.S. and 75¢ per book in Canada.* I understand that accepting the 2 free books and gifts places me under no obligation to buy anything. I can always return a shipment and cancel at any time. Even if I never buy another book, the two free books and gifts are mine to keep forever.

119/319 HDN GHWC

Name	(PLEASE PRINT)

Address	Apt. #

City	State/Prov.	Zip/Postal Code

Signature (if under 18, a parent or guardian must sign)

Mail to the **Reader Service**:
IN U.S.A.: P.O. Box 1867, Buffalo, NY 14240-1867
IN CANADA: P.O. Box 609, Fort Erie, Ontario L2A 5X3

Want to try two free books from another line?
Call 1-800-873-8635 or visit www.ReaderService.com.

* Terms and prices subject to change without notice. Prices do not include applicable taxes. Sales tax applicable in N.Y. Canadian residents will be charged applicable taxes. Offer not valid in Quebec. This offer is limited to one order per household. Not valid for current subscribers to Harlequin Romance Larger-Print books. All orders subject to credit approval. Credit or debit balances in a customer's account(s) may be offset by any other outstanding balance owed by or to the customer. Please allow 4 to 6 weeks for delivery. Offer available while quantities last.

Your Privacy—The Reader Service is committed to protecting your privacy. Our Privacy Policy is available online at www.ReaderService.com or upon request from the Reader Service.

We make a portion of our mailing list available to reputable third parties that offer products we believe may interest you. If you prefer that we not exchange your name with third parties, or if you wish to clarify or modify your communication preferences, please visit us at www.ReaderService.com/consumerschoice or write to us at Reader Service Preference Service, P.O. Box 9062, Buffalo, NY 14240-9062. Include your complete name and address.

HRLP15

READERSERVICE.COM

Manage your account online!
- Review your order history
- Manage your payments
- Update your address

> **We've designed the
> Reader Service website
> just for you.**

Enjoy all the features!
- Discover new series available to you, and read excerpts from any series.
- Respond to mailings and special monthly offers.
- Connect with favorite authors at the blog.
- Browse the Bonus Bucks catalog and online-only exculsives.
- Share your feedback.

Visit us at:
ReaderService.com